Together We Kill:

The Uncollected Stories of Mickey Spillane

Together We Kill:

The Uncollected Stories of Mickey Spillane

Mickey Spillane

Edited and with an introduction by
Max Allan Collins

Five Star • Waterville, Maine

Five Star First Edition Mystery Series.

Published in 2001 in conjunction with Tekno Books and Ed Gorman.

Cover art and design by Terry Beatty

Set in 11 pt. Plantin by Rick Gundberg.

Printed in the United States on permanent paper.

Library of Congress Cataloging-in-Publication Data

Spillane, Mickey, 1918–
    Together We Kill : the uncollected stories of Mickey
    Spillane / by Mickey Spillane ; edited and with an
    introduction by Max Allan Collins.
        p. cm.—Five Star first edition mystery series
    ISBN 0-7862-3560-3 (hc : alk. paper)
    1. Detective and mystery stories—American. I. Collins,
    Max Allan. II. Title.
    PS3537.P652 T58 2001
        813′.54—dc21   2001054489

Table of Contents

Together We Kill

an introduction
by Max Allan Collins

Mickey Spillane—the best-selling *noir* novelist of the Twentieth Century, the author of such seminal hard-boiled novels as *I, the Jury* (1948) and *Kiss Me, Deadly* (1952)—may well be a short story writer at heart. He cut his eyeteeth on the hard-boiled short fiction of Carroll John Daly and Fredric Brown, and honed his own craft in the pre-WWII comic book industry, writing short fiction "fillers" designed to satisfy certain postal regulations requiring text pieces. And though Spillane's famous detective Mike Hammer has appeared rarely in short stories, the Mick has frequently shown his affection for—and dexterity at—the short-fiction form, through periodic publication of such pieces as appear in this book.

Spillane in particular wrote short stories (and articles) for macho men's "mags" in the 1953–1960 period that his fans think of as the "drought" between novels (*Kiss Me, Deadly* in '52 and *The Deep* in '60). A number of these (often novellas) were collected in '60s paperbacks published by Corgi in Great Britain and Signet in the United States—Mickey needed quick money to fund his '62 film version of *The Girl Hunters*, in which he starred as Hammer—and most of the other stories were gathered in my 1984 Mysterious Press collection, *Tomorrow I Die.*

In the introduction to that book I mentioned that several

other stories—anthologized but never in a Spillane-only book—might be collected on another day. That day—a day of the guns, as Mickey would say—has arrived.

I also mentioned, in the intro to *Tomorrow I Die*, that I was still searching for unanthologized Spillane stories. My friend Lynn Myers—a true Spillane aficionado and historian—made an important discovery, not long ago: "Together We Kill," apparently the first of Spillane's fiction appearances in *Cavalier* magazine, unseen and unread—and unknown, even by so-called Spillane experts like myself—since 1953. The story proved to be terrific, and its typically Spillane title—melodrama wrapped up in a personal pronoun—gave a fitting name to this book.

Two of Spillane's best stories appear here; one of them, "Hot Cat," a short novel, is also known as "The Flier," and as such was the title story of a 1964 Great Britain paperback, never reprinted in the U.S.A. As published here, it contains an opening paragraph omitted from its publication in *The Flier*. "Hot Cat" reflects Mickey's love of flying, as does his personal favorite, "The Affair with the Dragon Lady" (his last *Cavalier* story), a rare, non-mystery valentine to the pilots of WWII (a group that includes Spillane).

Surprisingly, Mickey never really wrote Mike Hammer short stories. A few short works—a script for a "pilot" film ("The Screen Test of Mike Hammer," published in *Tomorrow I Die*) and a two-person playlet on a 1954 10" album, *Mickey Spillane's Mike Hammer Story*—almost qualify. And in recent years, Mickey has condensed his two latest Mike Hammer novels into short fiction form for *Playboy* (one of these, "The Killing Man," won a Private Eye Writers of America "Shamus" for best short story).

This book contains the only '50s vintage Hammer short story known to exist . . . and there's a tale behind the tale, as well. "The Night I Died" was a radio play manuscript I found in a corner of Mickey's office at his home in Murrell's Inlet, South Carolina. Though the story was in script form, Mike Hammer's distinctive voice-over made it possible to transcribe this typical Hammer yarn into short-fiction configuration . . . which I did, for the 1998 collection Mickey and I co-edited, *Private Eyes*.

"I'll Die Tomorrow" is another story Mickey wrote for *Cavalier*, a hitman tale that is one of his most overtly *noir* works. The two autobiographical short-shorts herein—"The Dread Chinatown Man" and "Toys for the Man-Child"—appeared in *True* in 1975, and pretty much bring to an end Mickey's long run as a contributor to macho men's magazines. "Hot Cat" had appeared in *Saga* in '64; around '62 Mickey had ceased contributing to *Cavalier* when its content shifted from blue-collar he-man subject matter—like sports cars and hunting—into pseudo-*Playboy* territory, with centerfolds and left-wing commentaries. Mickey never cared much for *Playboy*, and it's perhaps ironic that his most recent short stories have wound up there. *Cavalier*, by the way, makes a significant on-screen appearance in Spillane's film, "The Girl Hunters."

The most controversial Spillane story of all, "The Veiled Woman," is included here, as much for historical interest and completist purposes as any literary value. Spillane's only science-fiction work—at least until the revival of Mike Danger as a mid-'90s comic book with a futuristic setting—"The Veiled Woman" appeared in the second issue of *Fantastic*, to much fanfare. But did Mickey really write it?

Rumors—some of them spiteful ones by the likes of the late Michael Avallone, a gifted but troubled writer who envied Spillane's success—have abounded over the years that some of Mickey's work has been ghosted. Author Stephen

Marlowe was often cited as the author of several '60s Spillane novels. Mickey denies this vehemently, and Marlowe—in an interview for my documentary, "Mike Hammer's Mickey Spillane" (1999)—is just as adamant that he never ghosted anything for Mike Hammer's creator . . . though Marlowe did admit his own work owed Spillane a heavy debt.

The rumored author of "The Veiled Woman" is Howard Browne, a fine novelist and screenwriter and the author of the Paul Pine private eye novels, which are much admired. In the early '50s, Browne was the editor of *Fantastic* when Spillane's story was scheduled to appear. Browne had purchased an outline for the story from Mickey and advertised the tale heavily, at a time when Spillane's name carried the weight of Stephen King or Dean Koontz . . . at least.

But Mickey missed his deadline, and Browne—working from Spillane's proposal—quickly wrote a Spillane pastiche. When it appeared, Mickey was furious . . . but Browne explained the situation—that the young magazine had hyped the Spillane appearance and simply had to deliver to its readers—and Mickey withdrew his complaints.

I knew Browne fairly well, and spoke to him about this a number of times; and I know his tellings of the above varied as to detail. But this is how Browne explained "The Veiled Woman" to me, and it gibes with Mickey's explanation. So it appears in this, the companion volume to *Tomorrow I Die*, in an effort to complete the collected Spillane short fiction . . . and may be fairly viewed as a collaboration between two terrific writers, if the least of the tales in this book by some distance.

Is this, then, the final Spillane collection? Possibly not. Is this everything? Definitely not. My friend Lynn Myers and I are attempting to locate Spillane's short-shorts for the comic book market, and are already well on our way; also remaining

are wonderful Spillane articles on moonshine hot rodders, race car driving, deep-sea fishing and the circus, among others. We hope to gather these into a final volume, probably entitled *Byline: Mickey Spillane.*

And who knows what other Spillane gems may turn up, unexpectedly, like "Together We Kill"? Speaking of which, you're in for a real treat, reading that yarn, and its brothers, in the pages ahead, littered as they are with fliers, hitmen, private eyes and Mickey Spillane himself.

Max Allan Collins
June 14, 2001

Together We Kill

I avoided the street for six months; I kept the hell away from it all that time. Yet, I knew as sure as the grass grows green that the first time I set foot on it she'd be there. It wouldn't be something that she'd plan or I'd plan, no, nothing so simple as that. It would be that evil little fate that's followed me ever since the day I was born who would do it. Laughing, always laughing at me. A mean snicker I could hear, and my insides would go all in a knot again because there was nothing I could do about it.

Any other time I wanted to go west from Broadway I'd take some other street, but never this one. It was one block long, but only a little way off the corner was the theatre and her picture outside. Several pictures. That, and a long line of people demanding tickets for "Fair Is the Wind" and the chance to see the beauty that was Claire.

Every day she was there in magazines, newspapers, on billboards, beautiful and blonde with the loveliness of youth and maturity combined, exotically appealing and so alive with that radiance that comes only from the soul. And everybody wanted her. Hollywood screamed for her and Broadway wouldn't let her go. There was never a moment when she wasn't surrounded by men who fought for her smiles and who would give anything they owned for just the chance to touch her.

Claire was beauty. Claire was love. She was everything all women want to be and all men want.

But to me Claire was a memory. You see, I had Claire.

But that was seven years ago in a different world, and this was Broadway and there she was in front of me. If I hurried I knew I could catch her before she turned and went into the street level bistro, the one with the big wooden rooster hanging over the door.

But I didn't hurry, because even the sign of the rooster was part of the joke fate was playing. The Rooster was the place we promised to meet seven years ago. Now it was noon, and the Rooster was only a few doors from Claire's theatre and she was going there for lunch with never a thought of that last moment in France or of me. So I didn't hurry at all. I watched her go in and kept going past the theatre.

Now that I saw her, at last, I could forget her and all she'd done to me. I could go up to see Gus Kimball who had his office up the block and tell him to skip the whole deal. It was off, finished, kaput.

Four months ago he'd called me in and said, "Joe, we're putting that tunnel through in Bolivia. The engineer who's to tie the job together has to be tops. That guy is you. It's big money, and a chance to make a name for yourself, even a better one than you have now. How about it?"

That was a silly question. Does a bee want honey? I got one of those grins on my face that wouldn't wipe off because the world was in my lap. "You bought yourself an engineer, Gus."

He grinned back and poured a pair of shot glasses full. "We'll drink to it then. Frankly, Joe, I was worried for fear you wouldn't take it. It's a lonely place to be and you'll be there for a few years. In some respects it isn't *the* dream job."

"Nuts," I said. "For me it's beautiful."

13

"Fine, then there's only one other detail to iron out. You know the company policy. It may sound extreme, but we found that it works. All our company officers are required to take their wives on the job."

My grin was hard to hold. I threw the drink down fast.

"Not that I'm worried," he added. "Guys like you aren't without women . . . not from what I've heard about you. Aren't you engaged?"

"I was. Several times."

"Lucky you," he chuckled. "I wish I was thirty and on the brawny side again. Well, you have four months to get things settled. Stop in then and we'll go over the details and arrange for transportation of your personal effects. A woman needs a lot of pretty things down there to keep her morale up."

I said something I don't remember and we shook hands. That was four months ago. Helen and Jean and Gloria and Francis ago. All beautiful, all ready to share a life with me that couldn't be shared because Claire had been there before them and would always be there before anybody else. That was what my personal fate did to me—let me climb for the top on a ladder that was one big fat rung short.

But there was always the memory of having had her. I could reach back through the seasons to that time when St. Marie was nothing but a huddled mass of hills and houses on the ground below me, and when the moonlight filtered past the canopy of my parachute to sketch a fuzzy round shadow on the meadows. . . .

It was a bad night for the jump. It left you a dangling target for anybody who happened to look up, but it had to be that way. The bridge had to go. The push was due in the morning; a whole army was coming through the slot that had been opened up the day before. But the push wasn't a secret any

longer and the Krauts were moving up an army that could plug the hole. It depended on me, one guy with a sackful of high explosives strapped to his back, and a bridge over a river that ran through St. Marie.

When the bridge went, the Krauts went.

There was only the faintest whisper of sound when I hit the grass. I rolled with the fall and snagged the bottom shrouds to spill the air out of my chute, snatching up the lines and the nylon so the white blob wouldn't be there to give me away. I was tearing the sod away to bury it when the voice said, "No . . . m'sieu, not there!"

I went flat on my face, the .45 in my hand ready to spit when I saw her, a white face speaking to me from the folds of a cape. "You damn near died, girl," I told her. My hand and my voice shook together.

"I die every night, m'sieu. Come with me, please. If I saw you, then perhaps others saw you, too. Quickly."

She took my arm and led me away from the field to a footpath, then to a low stone house built into the side of the hill. I went in behind her and stood with my back to the door while she covered the windows and touched a match to the candle on the table. When she turned around she saw the gun in my hand still pointing at her stomach.

"I am not of . . . *them!*" She spit the word out.

"Maybe not, kid. It's just that I've seen all kinds of traps and I'm not taking any chances." I grinned at her because I was jumpy and didn't want her to know that I was scared, too.

She tossed off the cape. Maybe that's when I fell in love with her. It happened too fast, and all of a sudden I felt slippery inside and wanted to come apart at the seams. I thought a lot of things all at once, but most of all I thought what suckers war made of us, how it could make a man's mind forget what his body never stops remembering.

She was beautiful even then. Twenty maybe, soft and beautiful, with eyes that burned holes in your soul. Hell, you don't describe that kind of beauty. You have to think it or imagine it. Her body was the fulfillment of a dream, every movement more than a subtle invitation . . . a complete giving if you were *the* man. For anyone else it would be torture. I slid the gun back in the shoulder holster and stood there. She smiled and the room went bright.

"It is the bridge you want, is it not?"

I didn't answer her. She sat down quickly, her fingers drumming the table.

"We have known this would come. So have *they*." She spit it out again. "You will not be able to do it according to your plans, m'sieu. Only this afternoon they have brought in many men to guard the place. They are all over because the bridge is their only weak link. You see, they know."

"We found that out," I said.

"And your plans?"

I laughed. "To do it anyway." I started climbing out of my jump suit, stripping down until I was in ragged breeches and the torn shirt of a farmer. I tucked the gun in my belt and the explosives in a sack over my shoulder.

"You will be shot if you are caught, of course."

"Of course."

Her laugh was deep and throaty, a laugh of devilish amusement. "You Americans have too much of the . . . bravery. Sometimes you forget that one need not be so . . . direct. There are other ways of doing things and not getting shot."

I looked at her carefully, alive to the woman, yet alert to every sound that came through the night. From the village I could hear the rumble of trucks going over the pavement. "Who are you, girl?"

"In the underground I have a code number. Always, since I was a little girl, I have played under the bridge and along the banks of the river. When the people of the village moved I was directed to stay. You see . . . for long we knew that this time would come, and since I was the only one who was familiar with every spot that would be of importance about the bridge, the job was assigned to me. I am to . . . guide you, shall I say?"

"No, let's not say it. The thing's too pat."

"There is not time to argue. Certainly your intelligence knows how heavily the bridge has been guarded."

"They know it."

"Then how can I convince you that you must trust me?"

"You can't," I said. "It's still too pat. We never communicated with the French underground on this movement."

Her fingers stopped tapping the table. "I said we expected this. The railway is the only one on which troops can be moved. All the roads are out of service."

I said, "Sorry, kid," but I made it easy by backing it up with a smile.

"I see." Her eyes bored into mine, searching for the answer. "And what will you do with me?"

"Tie you up so you can get loose after a while. Like I said, there are too many traps for me to step in one blind."

A smile played with the corners of her mouth. It stayed a while then danced into her eyes. "I should curse you in the name of France for being so stupid. But too, I should curse myself and the others for being so cautious as not to leave any proof of my identity behind."

I had a coil of rope wound around my waist and I started to shake it loose. "In the name of France and the others you'll do better if you let me alone: I told you that I wasn't taking chances. The Krauts come across with nice prizes for dragging in a saboteur or two."

"And why couldn't I have turned you in before?"

I held the rope in my hand and fiddled with it. "Because I'm a man and you're a woman, chicken. A beautiful woman, but still a woman."

Her hand had a gun in it and it was aimed right at my head. My fingers jerked the rope tight and my mouth felt dry. "If I had wanted to I could have killed you before. Or I could have drawn a prize as you seem to think." She laid the gun on the table with the butt toward me. "Do you still think I shouldn't be trusted?"

The stiffness left my fingers and I wound the rope back around my waist. "Someday I'll smarten up," I said. When she saw that I wasn't going to touch the gun she put it back in the folds of her skirt. I glanced at her sharply. "You know what will happen if they catch you with that thing?"

"Yes. First I will kill several of them, then myself."

She meant it, every word of it. I finished tucking the ends of the rope in, then straightened up. "Okay, what gives. Tell me two things: if you knew how important the bridge was, why didn't the underground do something about it? When you tell me that tell me how we're going to go about it."

"The thing you carry in your pack is the thing we lacked. We have no explosive. Nor is it a job for one person."

"Why?"

"You'll see. As for the plans, they were arranged long ago. I told you that was why I was left behind."

"Go on."

"The war came close to us, m'sieu . . ."

"My name is Joe."

"And mine is Claire. As I said, the war came close. Rather than risk destruction the populace moved to the hills beyond."

"Not even token resistance?"

Her voice had a sharp edge. "It was hardly necessary. It happens that here we had the radio transmitters and the printing plants that was the lifeblood of the underground. We could not afford to have it captured."

"Sorry," I said. "You're brave."

Her eyes got grey and cloudy. "No braver than you, Joe. You expected to die when you came here, did you not?"

I shrugged my shoulders. "I figured it would happen sometime."

"It may not be necessary. You have made arrangements to be picked up?" I nodded a yes. "Then we shall hope for the best. However, it is agreed that I will lead you there?"

I was doing everything I shouldn't do. I was taking a chance on an unknown quantity in violation of all my training. How many lives depended on my judgment—thousands? All because a woman was beautiful, with a deep, rich voice and eyes that burned holes into my soul. I was fully briefed to do my job, yet here I was letting a woman change plans that had been made by experts.

And I knew I was right, I knew it damn well! I looked at my watch, and said, "Let's go."

The bridge is part of history now, but not that night. That's pure screaming torture that has etched itself into my memory with an acid so strong it will never leave. I could forget it, if within an hour I hadn't found myself loving her and having it returned.

But it happened and I can't forget it, see? She was mine. She was beautiful and soft, and she was mine before the moon was at its peak. . . .

That night the air and the ground were alive with death. We heard the sharp metallic noises it made and felt the force of it waiting to thunder into reality. It was there in light and shadows, and we walked through it safely. Claire took my hand and I responded to the slightest pressure of her touch, letting her show me the path until we had the sounds behind us and the sound of the river coming our way.

We still had two hours to wait, timing ourselves so the job could be completed with precious minutes left over for me to reach the field where the plane would come down.

We didn't speak of our plans. Somehow we both knew what was to be done, and whatever she had to do I didn't want to know about.

That was where we found life, there right in the middle of death. We forgot about it and talked of the things that were and would still be when it was over, lying on our backs facing the stars. I was counting them when a shadow of golden hair moved across my vision and I tasted the warmth of her mouth and the sweetness of her breath. She said, "We love each other, Joe."

My answer was in my arms and in the present. I had to come across a continent to find her. I was hers until the hands on my watch marked the time to end the life we had found.

After she was mine she took me to the banks of the river, leading the way through the weeds. She was calm, but I didn't dare speak. Along the causeway and on the bridge itself I could see the file of the sentries back and forth. They shouted instructions and commands, following any object that moved with the white beam of the searchlights. Then there would be the short snarl of the machine guns and the questions asked afterward. Nothing moved and lived.

"Notice, Joe . . ." I turned my head to her. "The river flows under the bridge, but here starts a little offshoot of the river that winds through the rushes. The bottom is clay, and if you walk softly without splashing and keep in the shadow of the tall grass, you can get under the bridge. From above this

20

looks like part of the bank and they will not be watching.
Their lights are trained on the river itself and the road along
the bank. Only in this one section of the river is the footing
solid enough to follow. None of them are under the bridge because no man can stand long in the ooze of the silt without
sinking under."

I nodded, picking out the way with my eyes, glad that the
moon was directly above, so that I'd leave no trailing shadow.
"I may not be able to be quiet."

Her voice was very soft. "They will not hear you, Joe."

"Why?" My chest felt tight.

"Because I am beautiful. Because I am the only woman in
the village and they are men, Joe. Kiss me once more."

I kissed her. I tried to crush the life out of her so nothing
would take her away from me, but she was too strong and
pulled back with a sad smile. "Always I will love you, Joe,"
she said.

There were only seconds left now. "No matter where I am
I'll be loving you, Claire. Remember this, the present doesn't
last long. When it's over I'll be looking for you, if we can live
through it. It might take a while to find you because even in
peace there are problems. I can't give you much, but it will be
more than you ever had before. If I can't get to you, try to
come to me. Right off Broadway there's a tiny bistro. A red
rooster hangs outside the door and we'll meet there. No
matter where I am, I'll come back on this day, the ninth of
each month, looking for you."

"I'll remember, Joe." Then she was gone. A white shadow
that simply disappeared. I shifted the sack of explosives and
stepped into the stream.

A cat couldn't have been more silent. I left nothing to re-
veal my passage through the brush. Not even a splash or the
snapping of a twig. Sure, I made it. No trouble at all because

she was right all along the line. It was a snap getting under the bridge and it left me feeling good because there was nothing to it. The boys back in HQ better get their medals ready, I kept thinking.

It made nice thinking, until I got a good look at the under-side of the structure, then I felt like a jerk. There was a key-stone there that would pull the whole works down, but getting up to it meant a scramble and a lot of noise. Swell. Just one lousy sound and I'd be dead. You know what I felt like. Not too far south a thousand guys could figure on dying because the job was too big for me. Maybe one of those guys was somebody *you* knew. Then you know how I felt.

Twenty feet above me the muted noises of soldiers on guard sounded like the drone of bees, never loud enough to muffle foreign sounds. I couldn't wait any longer. I shook my rope out and stood ready to throw it over the projecting beam above. One lousy sound and I'd die. Nice.

It didn't come. Like everything else I froze because the only other sound in the night was a deep, rich voice lifted in song. Somebody barked an order and the lights came around. Two of them. They pointed down river and merged on the banks where she stood so lovely and white and naked.

Somebody choked out a whistle.

She dived into the water, flashed to the surface and shook her hair back from her face, then swam to the shore again, framed in the lights that never left her, laughing and waving toward the bridge.

Sound? Who could have heard me? There was so much sound that I whistled while I tied the explosive into place and set off the long fuse. They screamed from the rail, whistled and shouted to that vision so tantalizingly close to them, yet so far out of reach. Hell, I even laughed too.

Yeah, I laughed. I finished the job and got away.

I made the field where the plane picked me up, but the laugh was a frozen grimace of hate and fury because I'll never forget the light picking up the officers throwing their clothes on the banks and diving in after her. She swam away, her arms flashing in the light, laughing over her shoulder, letting them draw closer and closer so every eye on the bridge was focused on the wanton sight, their eager shouts and cheers drowning out the noise of my escape and the sputtering of the fuse and even the sound of the light plane taking off again from the field.

And from the air I could see the bright fingers of the light trained on the banks of the river now, and I said, "Oh, God! Oh, God!" and I thought I could hear their laughter even up there. Then when the flash came there was nothing. No noise. Just that one intense glare and I went on into the night. Later, I wondered if she gave all that for me or for her country. I tried to joke about it. It wasn't funny. Not even to myself.

I saw her again. Sure, so did you. Beauty didn't die that easily. The present went and the future came after it. The world settled back and enjoyed the beauty that had been hidden by the war, and you saw a star come out of France that was a bright light of fame and fortune that glittered from the stage.

Those soldiers on the bridge weren't the only ones she drove mad. Whenever you saw her picture you saw someone staring at it with that funny look on his face. Everybody wanted her and she had everything she wanted. What was it I was going to take her away from—the poverty that was Europe? That was another laugh.

The price of a necklace she wore at a premiere was more

than I could save in five years. It was a real big laugh, a regular howl, because I could go through a succession of Helens and Jeans and Frans and it was Claire who kept them out. Claire, the memory.

So she wound up in New York, the hit of the year's biggest play. And she ate at the bistro with the sign of the rooster over the door, but that was only because it was noon and time for lunch and it was only a few doors away from the theater. . . .

I started past the door for my appointment with Gus Kimball and then I got curious. Hell, I thought, why be a dope? Any guy likes to shake hands with fame, and maybe she'd remember me if she thought hard enough. I wouldn't prod her with unpleasant memories. That's what the psychiatrists would say. Go in and face your problem, and then you'll have nerve enough to walk up the street again without going all shaky inside.

I opened the door and stepped in. Henri hadn't seen me for years, but his memory was good. He said, "Why, good afternoon, Joe! It is good to have you back. A table, yes?"

"No, Henri, not right now." I was looking across the room. "I just came in to speak to somebody a moment."

My feet pulled me through the tables. She was by herself off in a corner and didn't see me until I was in front of her. "Hello, kid," I said.

"Joe." Just like that, "Joe." That's all she said.

I pulled a cigarette out and stuck a light to it. Funny, but my hand didn't shake. I blew the smoke toward the ceiling and grinned at her. "Imagine us crossing again. Didn't think you'd remember me. I saw you turn in here and had to come in to be sure. You look good."

"Do I?" I damned Henri for not having more lights in the place. I couldn't see her face very well.

"Yeah. You did all right for yourself, too. I see your name

24

in the papers every day. How do you like our country?"

"I like it, Joe."

She hadn't moved. Now that I was in the dark a while, after the brightness of the street, I began to see the vague outline of her face. The fires started inside of me and I couldn't let them do it to me again. Not any more.

"Well, I got an appointment, kid. Maybe one day I'll look you up if you're not too busy. I have to go now."

People were looking over at us, and I thought I saw her teeth bite her lips. Maybe she was thinking back to those searchlights.

She stood up quickly, scooping her handbag under her arm. What the hell, I didn't blame her a bit. Nobody famous wants to be hamstrung by something from a forgotten past.

"It is I who has to go, Joe," she said. Then she was gone.

Henri stood at my elbow. "You were to have lunch with the lady?"

"No, Henri. I was just saying hello."

"A strange woman, Joe. Always she comes in once a month and sits here. Always the same day, the ninth of each month. It is that she has a pact, perhaps?"

The fires wouldn't go out. The cigarette fell from my fingers and scattered sparks on the floor. The tight knot inside me jerked even tighter and something was going on in my head, fighting and screaming to free itself. Something that didn't sound like my voice said. "And today, Henri . . . ?"

"Is the ninth, Joe."

I ran. I pushed everything aside and I ran, and if I went fast enough I could catch her before she disappeared again, and I could tell Gus that the job was fine and I'd be there with bells on. Wedding bells.

I caught her.

25

The Night I Died

A Mike Hammer Story

You walk down the street at night. It's raining out. The only sound is that of your own feet. Then you hear another sound and you look across the street and see the blonde.

The blonde.

The girl you've been looking for for two whole years. She's blonder now. A little bit heavier but on her it's okay. And more beautiful than ever. She had to be more beautiful than ever. The girl you've been looking for for two years but never wanted to see again in your life.

So you follow her for a little while, then out of force of habit that's two years old, you cross the street and stay behind her. Yeah, even from there she hadn't changed. All the grace of a cat was in her walk and maybe some of their animal instincts, too.

Maybe she heard me.

Maybe she just felt me.

That's the way it always had been. Her steps got slower and shorter then she stopped altogether and there was Helen.

Lovely, lovely Helen who I loved so much—but was going to kill in just another minute.

The gun in my pocket that had gotten warm from my hand felt cold all of a sudden. Cold and almost too heavy to lift, but

26

I got it out of my pocket and had it in front of me when I reached her. She still had those deep green-tinted eyes that could laugh at you . . . even when you were dying . . . and now it was Helen who was dying and she could still laugh.

"Hello, Helen."

A long pause. "Hello, Mike. Do I get it here?"

"That's right. Here, Helen. Just like I said it would be. The next time I ever saw you, wherever it was . . . and now it's here."

"All right, Mike."

"It won't hurt much, but I'm not worried about that kind of pain. What I want you to feel will be right inside your mind. A slow, agonizing pain that wants to scream but can't make a sound because it's all inside you. It's life screaming because death is catching up with it . . . and all you'll be able to do is lie there listening to that silent screaming and the last thing you'll hear will be my feet walking away."

"Not even a kiss good-bye, Mike?"

"Not even a kiss good-bye. The last one was two years ago. That one will hold me. . . . That was a real kiss . . . a real kiss of death. *Remember it, Helen?*"

Sure she remembered it. How could she ever forget it? The kiss of death. Hers. Two years ago was the night I died. But there was a time before that . . . many nights before. The time we met.

There was a party going on. You know the kind . . . all the Broadway wheels spilling champagne and someplace in the background a soft piano setting the mood. I said my hellos but I didn't like the people I was forced to associate with and was ready to leave when I saw her. . . .

There was loneliness in her . . . loneliness and something else that didn't belong there. Fear. The kind of fear that

27

didn't belong at a party like this one, with a crowd like this one.

Then our eyes met over the heads of everybody and suddenly the room seemed to empty slowly until there was nobody there or even in the whole world except the two of us.

And fear.

I walked over to her . . . looked at her and could feel my spine get crawly.

"I came alone," I said.

"So did I."

"Then you're with me."

I didn't expect the mist that flowed into her eyes. A wisecrack maybe, but anything except the mist.

"For how long?" she asked.

"Forever?"

She paused. "I think . . . I wish it could be . . . forever."

"Let's get out of here."

Her scared cry overlapped my words: *"No!"*

"What's scaring you?"

That surprised her.

"Yeah—it shows, kid." I paused. "Let's get out, girl. Nobody'll ever bother you while I'm there. I'm funny that way."

"Forever?"

"Maybe forever. We have to start sometime."

So we went, the two of us . . . and fear. Fear that was there when she told me her name was Helen Venn, fear that was with us in a cab and stayed like an invisible shroud when we walked through the park.

"It's a pretty night, Mike."

"Maybe."

She turned her head and looked at me, the swirl of her hair a golden waterfall in the moonlight.

"There's something wrong with your eyes, Mike."

"Yeah, I know. They don't look at you . . . they watch you. That what you mean?"

"That's right. What are they watching?"

"A kid in trouble. It's all over you. Why, Helen?"

"It's quite a story." She hesitated. "I think . . . Mike!"

Footsteps ran toward us, jostled into us, but the dark shape veered off, into the mess of shrubs. I ran after him, but he was gone.

"He got away," I said, breathing hard.

"Please don't go after him!"

"Don't worry. I couldn't find him in there anyway. Look . . . remember I said this could be . . . forever?"

"I remember."

"Then we go someplace and sit down. We'll hear some music and you can talk to me. Whatever it is, I want to hear it all."

So we went someplace and talked, a little place with soft lights—softer music. Then she told me.

"There isn't too much, Mike, but what there is . . . well, it's deadly. Look at me. Big, beautiful . . . even educated. Some might say I'm lucky. But I'm not. I'm just one of thousands more like me who are caught in this . . . rat trap of New York. Then I met a man. He was quite a guy. I went head over heels for the dirty . . . him. Then he was killed. Shot. It was only then that I found out who he was. Marty Wellman."

"Marty. *He* was your guy. . . . That slob was the biggest hood the Syndicate ever turned out."

"I know that now. Do you know why he was killed?"

"Sure. Someplace he had a couple of tax-free millions stashed away. It's a good reason for murder."

"Now do you know why I'm scared?"

"Tell it to me."

29

"They . . . or whoever the killer is thinks I know where it is." She paused. "Mike . . . I'm tired of being afraid. I'm tired of walking the street afraid to look back and more afraid to look ahead. I'm tired of looking at my front door night after night, waiting for it to open slowly until I see a killer standing there with a gun in his hand. Mike . . . I'm tired, do you understand? Tired of living . . . afraid of living anymore. Mike . . . I want to die. I want to so bad I'm going to do it myself. I'm . . ."

"Shaddup!"

"No! I . . ."

"Shaddup, I said."

She did.

"I'll get him for you, girl. He'll never bother you again. He'll never bother anybody again."

"The police . . . they never . . ."

"I'm not the police."

"Then . . . it still might be . . . forever, Mike?"

"We can make it go however we want it to go. But I'll need some help from you."

"You can have . . . anything you want from me, Mike."

And forever started that night.

It started when Helen took me to the place Marty Wellman used to run, a smooth bistro catering to the uptown trade that ran as far as up to Ossining on the Hudson. Those who were popular that far up made the backroom a gambler's paradise and a sucker's grave.

No, she wouldn't come in. She stayed in the cab and that's the way I wanted it. There was muted music and indirect lighting. The coatroom was jam-packed but there wasn't a dozen people at the bar. The rest were digging their graves behind the curtain alongside the bandstand.

30

I walked up to the bar and sat down.

"Yessir," the bartender said.

"Gimme a beer."

"Yessir!"

He brought the beer and moved away.

"Hey, feller. Come here a minute."

"Yeah?"

"How long have you been here?"

"About two years."

"You knew Marty Wellman, then, didn't you?"

"Yeah, I knew Marty."

"*What* did you know about him?"

"Nothing."

"Don't walk away, friend."

He paused. "Friend . . . look. If you're just a wise guy . . . get out by yourself. If you're a tough guy I'll toss you out. You know?"

"Friend . . . *look.*"

I held my coat open just enough so he could see the leather of the sling that ran across my chest. I didn't have to show him the .45 that was under it.

"I'm a tough guy, friend. Real tough. Different from the other kind. I'll tell you my name. Just once. Then you talk . . . understand. It's Mike . . . Mike Hammer."

"Yeah. . . ."

"Who owns the place now, friend?"

"Me . . . I do. There's my license on the wall."

"Swell. Who runs it?"

"Me . . . I—"

"Friend . . . from where you stand maybe I don't look mad enough to do it, but you're going to be hurting awful bad with a slug in your leg."

"Ease off, will you, I'm trying to tell you . . ."

"Never mind, Joe," another voice said. "We'll tell him."

Whatever the guy behind me had in his pocket pressed hard against my back. The bartender tried to grin but it looked a little sick.

"Much trouble, Joe?" the guy asked.

"Not too much, Dave. He's got a gun."

"He won't have it long. Get up slow, bud. You know where to go or should I steer you a little?"

That was a laugh. Go? I could find it with my eyes closed. Sure, I went . . . nice and orderly, too . . . through the crowd at the wheels, around the dice tables, then up to the door marked private and I didn't even have to knock.

There were four of them in there . . . plus a languid red-head. But only one of them counted.

His name? Sure, you remember him . . . Carmen Rich. The boy with all the muscles. The rising star in the world that lived at night. You heard of Buddy Whiteman, too, the slick gunslinger from Miami who was always at Carmen's arm. And now there they were.

"This the guy?" Carmen asked.

"Troublemaker at the bar," Dave said.

"They never learn, do they?"

"Not until we teach them, Carmen."

"Maybe you got a good idea of what's going to happen to you, feller. You want to speak, say it now."

"You slimy thick-necked jerk," I said. "You scrimey punk . . ."

"Take him, Buddy. Take him good."

"Yeah, take me," I said. "But before you start, remember something. There's a gun at my back but there's one under my arm and I can get it out a second before I die and in that one second I can plant a slug between your eyes and maybe

32

the Miami boy too and if living is that cheap to you, go ahead and take me."

Nobody moved.

They sat there watching me . . . and they knew. That kind could always tell.

Carmen said, "Hold it, Buddy. . . . What's the angle?"

I laughed. "Me . . . and a dead man. Marty Wellman. Why did he die? Who killed him? There's your angle."

"I'll pay for that information," Carmen said.

"So will a killer."

"I don't get you, guy."

"Nobody ever does."

"Have a cigarette?"

"No thanks. I'll stick to my Camels."

Carmen clicked his lighter, puffed his cigarette. "Why'd you come here?"

"Let's say to see you. The guy at the bar owns the joint and you run it. So Marty left a will."

"That's right. Marty left a will."

"You don't leave a gambling concession in a will, Carmen."

"You know me?"

"Yeah. And you know me, too. Mike Hammer. Maybe you heard."

Carmen paused. "I heard."

Whiteman said, "I hate these big-mouthed characters. Let me take him, Carmen."

"I'd like to see you try it, Buddy," Carmen said. "It'd be real funny. He'd actually die just to pump one into both of us."

"Nuts," Buddy said.

"Buddy . . ." Carmen said. "If you try it . . . I'll kill you my-self. I know this guy."

33

"He's pulling a bluff and . . ."

"*I'm* not, Buddy," Carmen said. "I've seen some of the dead men he left behind him."

"So you know why I'm here," I said. "You have any answers?"

"You should know the story," Carmen said. "Someplace Marty had money stashed away. Two million is a good haul."

"Where, Carmen?"

"Would I run this joint if I knew?"

"Okay," I said. "I was just asking. Now I'll ask around other places. You better be on the square, feller. Otherwise I'll be back."

I pulled away from the guy behind me. "Hey . . . what is this?" he said.

"Let him go, Dave," Carmen said.

I laughed and shut the door on them.

A croupier was calling out as I slid my barstool into place. "Hey, friend . . . gimme a beer."

"Yessir, what can I . . ."

The bartender's eyes were wide.

I said, "They didn't do it to me, feller."

"I don't get it," the bartender said softly.

"You will, feller . . . if you work that buzzer behind the bar on me again. I said I was different from the other kind of tough guy. You know?"

"Yeah," the bartender said, dragging it out.

"I'm getting out now . . . Just remember me if I ever come back."

Sometimes it's good to be a guy who doesn't have to worry about the rules. You can learn things that are clubs to hold over somebody's head and you can prowl the night until you find the ferrets . . . human animals who live by invading the dens of the rats.

But first I went to a rat.

He was dressed in grey from his head to his shoes. His hair was mousy color and his eyes were the kind you see peering out of holes in the wall.

Sid Pollack was a rat. On his paper they called him a columnist, but a lot more on the outside called him a rat. He was living by night in a gin mill on Third Avenue that had taken on the taint of respectability lately.

"Hi, Sid."

"What do *you* want, Hammer?"

"You."

"Scram."

"There was a court case. There was a witness. There was a big lie told and a stinking murderer got off free." I paused. "There was a night a week later when the killer called on the witness and passed over an envelope with ten grand in it."

His voice was hushed. "You dirty . . ."

"Shut up or I'll break your back right over the bar stool."

"What do you want?"

"News. Who runs the Syndicate since Marty Wellman got hit?"

"You ought to know."

I just looked at him.

"Okay . . . lay off," he said hurriedly. "So it's Carmen Rich."

"How?"

"He moved in. There's another way?"

"Not without an army, there isn't."

Sid smirked. "He's got an army."

"Yeah?"

The reporter spoke slowly, with contempt. "You crazy

35

fool. He's got Buddy Whiteman. He's got a kill-batty jerk who'll knock off the whole town if he says so. The Miami Kid is the fastest thing you ever saw with a rod. You stick your head out. I'll be giving you a two-line obituary in my column and glad to do it."

"Why haven't the cops tagged Buddy Whiteman?"

He laughed. "The cops. The only thing they haven't got to hit him with is evidence, you jerk you. Maybe after you . . ."

I slapped him.

He dropped his glass and stopped laughing.

"Don't ever laugh at me, Sid."

The cops? No, don't fool yourself. They don't make any mistakes. They're good boys to keep on the right side of. One in particular. Meet him yourself. His name is Pat Chambers . . . Captain of Homicide. We were buddies, so I could speak to him. We were buddies, so he could speak to me.

"You know, Mike," Pat said, "if anybody but you asked me for information on Wellman, Rich, or Whiteman, I'd hold them for questioning. What are you up to?"

"That isn't an answer."

"First *you* tell *me* things."

"A woman is slowly dying because a killer is loose. I like that woman."

Pat paused. "Helen Venn?"

"You're a brain, Pat. It's her."

"Be careful, friend. She's marked."

"I know."

"We kept a tail on her after Marty's death. She's marked. . . . We know that . . . but we don't know how, why, or by whom."

"The paper never said much about Marty catching it."

He threw the sheaf of papers on his desk; they scattered.

"There's the file on him. A few pictures, too. That one there is the last he ever had taken."

It was a police photo, a garish head-on shot of Marty Wellman, the muscle kid. Too handsome for his own good. Too big and broad for anybody else's good either.

He looked pretty sharp sitting there at his desk in a dressing gown that was open to let his chest hair show through. His head was turned to one side and a cigar was tight in his pretty teeth.

Yeah, pretty sharp. The only trouble was that he was pretty dead, too. The bullet hole showed right over his ear.

".38 slug did it," Pat said.

"He got it cold?"

"No . . . warm, sort of. The desk drawer was open and a snub-nosed .38 was right where he could get it. Notice his hand. It's still lying almost on the rod. He must have sat there with the thing in his hand."

"It was a hard two million he had, Pat."

"I'll tell you something, kid. We found out about that. The two million was a bluff. He never had it. He called that bluff his insurance dough for retirement and used it to bank himself into control of the Syndicate's gambling setup in town here."

"Some use money . . . some use a bluff . . . and some use an army."

"What?"

"Nothing . . . Helen Venn. What about her?"

"Beautiful . . . and lonely. Marty cultivated her. That was another bluff, only she didn't know it."

"I'm glad he's dead."

"Oh, it wasn't all his fault. You know dames. If she hadn't been looking for a push ahead, she wouldn't have hung out with the money boys. First it was Earnie Haver. Then Salvy

Slocum. Big Ed Smith got in line and finally it was Marty. She was quite a girl to get a yen for."

"Yeah."

"You say it funny, Mike."

"Yeah. Was she really a pusher, Pat?"

"Oh . . . I wouldn't say so. A kid blinded by the bright lights, let's say. She checked clean."

"Do we talk about the Syndicate?"

"Do you mean Carmen Rich?"

"That's right."

"No, we don't talk."

"Carmen too big to talk about?"

"Let's stay friends, kid."

"Sorry," I said.

"We don't talk because it's a sealed case. It's being worked on."

"Okay, Pat, thanks." I stood. "I'll dig around. Anything turns up . . . I'll buzz *you*."

"Swell," he said. "Do that."

I had asked rats first. They didn't know. Then the cops. They wouldn't talk. There were still the ferrets . . . sharp-eyed little people who walked in the shadow of the rats and knew everything they did. All you had to do was get them to open their mouths.

On the Bowery I found my ferret.

He was sleeping in a doorway dreaming big dreams and living under a blue sky someplace that was warm and comfortable. . . . He didn't like it too much when I woke him up.

"Hello, Jake."

"Hey . . . hey . . . cut it."

"It's me, kid—Mike Hammer."

He scrambled to his feet, scared.

"Come here, come here . . . what's the matter with you?"

"Look, lemme alone, Mike. Just lemme alone."

I held his arm and hauled him in close until the sour whiskey smell of him was right under my nose.

"What's the matter with you? You want a fin or a train ticket? I'm not too good to speak to, am I?"

He groaned loudly. "Mike . . . look, lemme say it fast. . . . The word's out. They're gunning for you. You ain't healthy no more."

"Who?"

"Who knows? The word's out. Mike . . . lemme go."

"Sure, Jake. Just answer me something. Why did Marty Wellman die?"

A long hiss escaped his lips. He was scared. "Mike!"

"Why, Jake . . . *why?*"

"There's talk . . . it isn't loud talk because if it gets heard somebody gets killed. Marty . . . he had to die. You know, the king is dead. Long live the king. He got pushed because somebody else wanted in."

"Carmen?"

"Honest, Mike, I . . ."

"Okay, I won't push you. But the talk I heard had two million bucks in it."

"Marty was flat. He borrowed fifty grand from a Chicago outfit. That sound like two million?"

"No." I gave him a fin. "Here—buy yourself a steak."

"Thanks."

And that was all the ferret had to say. No . . . he wouldn't have said another word. He was one more guy the fear had gotten to.

So now the word was out.

Somebody wanted . . . me.

"Don't move, mister," a voice said.

My boy Dave from the bar. The second time he held a gun on me.

"Sucker," he said. "Sucker. You would've had it easy if you didn't nose around. Come on."

"Where?"

"There's a car over there."

"Suppose I don't?"

"Try it."

"Yeah . . . yeah."

He wasn't fast enough.

Somebody should've told him. This is New York. You let them find out for themselves here. I stepped past him, .45 in hand, hearing the last little sounds he was making, aware of the complete silence that hung over the Bowery while a hundred eyes saw a kill that a hundred mouths would never speak about except among themselves.

But the dead man proved a point. I was important. Then I knew just how important. . . .

Important enough for two more of Carmen's boys to be on top of me, and I never saw the other one. I heard the swish and thud of the sap. . . .

"We can't go out to the island," a voice was saying.

"Then use the park," another voice said. "We can pull over, dump him, and blow."

"Suppose somebody hears the shot?"

"For the kind of dough we're making, you want Social Security?"

"Aw, shut up."

"Here's the place. Pull over."

They carried me out. They dragged me through the bushes and around a jutting tooth of rock like you find in Central Park, then they dumped me. The fat boy pulled the gun from his pocket, checked the shells, then flipped the cylinder back. . . .

I played it just a little too slow. Too slow. The louse got me with the gun butt and I had it good . . . just long enough to hear them get away.

But I wasn't too bad off. One dead man earlier still told the story. I started to get up . . . then my hand closed around a flat little pad and I thought how I had missed it earlier when I had chased somebody else into these same bushes . . . somebody who had been waiting for Helen and me ripped it out of his coat pocket when he tried to get me off his back.

I wrapped my handkerchief around it, stuck it in my pocket, and got up. It wouldn't take long to reach the street . . . or get a boy to run my package up to Pat's office.

It was enough for the night. Enough. I called a cab over and gave the driver Helen's address. . . .

"Hello, Mike," she said. "It's so good to see you."

"Helen . . . You look different, kid."

"I . . . *feel different,* Mike. I'm . . . not afraid anymore."

"You'll never have to be afraid again."

"But . . . you look different, too, Mike."

"Somebody else told me that once, too. They said they could always tell when I killed somebody."

"Mike! You killed . . ."

"What difference does it make. The pressure's off you now. They turned the heat my way." I hesitated. "You're beautiful, kid. Why? Why?"

"Why what, Mike?"

"Why do I love you so fast? What happens to a guy to make it so quick? Why, Helen? Why did a guy have to die tonight? Why is it I love you so much?"

"Maybe it's because I can love, too. I thought I loved be-

41

fore . . . but it wasn't like this. Nothing like this at all. I don't have to . . . work to love you, Mike. It's just there. It's something that makes you and me the only two people in the world. Something that is life and living . . . and love. Love . . . it makes fear seem so small and pitiful. When you love like this there isn't any room left for fear at all. Mike . . . remember you said forever?"

"Uh-huh."

"And I said I'd do anything in the world for you?"

"Yeah. . . ."

"And you said forever had to start sometime?"

"And forever starts . . ."

"Tonight, Mike."

Then you come into the mist once more because there's a killer loose and you're ready to start again. It's a day and a night later, and another day and a night and all along the way voices whisper to you while you wait.

They're after you, Mike.

Hey, Mike . . . watch it.

Pal . . . pal . . . a guy with a rod . . . he was here before . . .

And you listen without answering . . . but you listen. You see them. You know their faces . . . faces that are all alike . . . faces of hunters . . . but you move too fast . . . then you're ready to move and you watch and wait for a long time before you have him right.

He comes out of a building finally . . . and for the first time he's alone. You say . . .

"Carmen . . ."

Then he spins around and while the crazy feat is still on his face and the scream in his throat, there's a crashing thunder of a shot. . . .

And Carmen Rich fell with the blood, a wild angry stream

spurting from his throat, and you know the party isn't over yet. . . .

So you run and run until you're in the clear and stand there panting your lungs out . . . then another long day and then you begin to wonder and at last you get an idea . . . and see Pat again.

He spoke slowly, softly: "Mike . . . all I know is what they let me know. Sure Carmen is dead. They all die sooner or later, but someone's ready to fill in. No matter what the papers or the politicians say, we can't stop the Syndicate from operating."

"Who filled in, Pat?"

"I wish I knew. I wish I knew."

"Guess."

"Somebody who's here now. A million-dollar enterprise doesn't go without a president for long. But who? I don't know yet. By the way . . . the prints we lifted from that pad of yours. They belong to a guy named Ben Liter. Small-time hood. Mostly petty raps. What's the pitch?"

I snorted.

"Something?" he asked.

"No . . ." I said. "No . . . nothing, Pat."

Nothing. Always nothing. Even the voices that whispered told me nothing. In a way it was funny, all of it . . . from a bartender who owned a bar worth a fortune . . . but didn't run the business . . . to dead me . . . to guys in the bushes . . . to a new president. Toast. The king is dead. Long live the king. Ahhhh.

The queen.

Helen.

Tonight was rain and Helen and tomorrow the king could live and die but tonight was the queen . . . and live.

So I went back to the apartment. I got out of the cab. It was quiet . . . dark . . . and late, so that's why I heard him . . . and maybe why I followed him. Then there he was, going into the same building as I was. . . .

"Buddy!" I said.

He took two shots at me and I clawed my .45 out from under my arm and took pursuit.

And there we were, alone in the darkness, the back fences of the alleys crowding us, the rain a muffler that blanked out sound but we each knew the other was there and someplace where I could hear him breathing was the new king who was ready to kill my queen and for the first time I was the white knight and I laughed. . . .

"Buddy . . . you won't get out alive."

"You're kidding, feller. You're just kidding. You know who did it to Carmen? You know *why?*"

"Yeah," I said.

"Carmen was too big too long. I been small long enough. It's my turn now. I'm going up. Then you know what? I got everything I ever wanted. *Everything.* Nobody . . . understand . . . nobody . . . gets in my way. Nobody stops me or gets in my way even. Not you, nobody." He laughed. "Not even Mata Hari."

"They were big dreams, Buddy," I said. "You've had it."

"No," he said. "*You* get it. You and anybody in my way."

There was just that one exploding pain in my belly that smashed me into the ground . . . hard, wet, and the breath was gone for long seconds. There was that fuzzy feeling that I had known once, a long time ago in the stinking jungles of a Pacific island . . . but even then it hadn't been this bad . . . and then the king stood over me to put the final one in my head.

He shouldn't have been so gracious. . . .

His laugh was a whisper as he came over and he was still laughing when I shot him.

You could hear sirens someplace . . . they faded as I stood up, stopped altogether as I walked and all the sound I could hear was the rushing waterfall in my ears . . . but somehow I got up to her apartment . . . opened it with the key she had given me and staggered in.

My queen was beautiful . . . beautiful . . . standing there in that single light. Beautiful and mine.

And I was dying. . . .

"Mike?" Her voice was querulous.

"They're dead, Helen. It's one way of stopping the fear."

"Dead?"

"Carmen Rich . . . he didn't matter. Buddy Whiteman." I paused. "He mattered. He's dead, Helen, but I'm the only one who knows. You'll never have to be afraid of anything again. I'm the only one who knows."

"Mike . . . ?"

"The death photo of Marty Wellman. He had his hand on a gun, so he was afraid of a killer. But his head was turned to look at something else. Even with a killer in front of him, you'd be the only one he'd look at. The only thing he'd take his eyes off a killer for. And one other thing. It was small and wouldn't mean much except to me. The guy who watched us in the park . . . he was a small-timer. A guy with services for rent . . . but not to a big organization like the Syndicate, Helen. To you, maybe, but not the Syndicate."

"Yes . . . it was me, Mike. Me and Marty at first, but he wouldn't give me what I had earned. He had to die. You know that, don't you? Carmen?" She shook her head. "He wasn't the strong one I needed. I wanted someone who could act . . . quickly, decisively. Someone who could respond to my . . .

love . . . without anyone knowing it. Someone ready to do whatever I asked him to . . . no questioning . . . nothing." She shrugged. "That was Buddy Whiteman. The Miami Kid, they called him."

"Forget them, honey," I said. "It's over now. There's only you and me . . . for a few minutes at least."

"Mike . . . there's not even a few minutes. I'm scared again. I wanted so much. I almost had it . . . then I did have it . . . for a little bit. Mike . . . I'm going to have it for all time. I'm going to have the world at the snap of my fingers. Not a little bit . . . everything! Buddy killed Carmen for me." She laughed shortly. "He was going to kill you, too. Mike . . . you see, here's how it is. Buddy got ambitious, too. That was the sad part of it. He and I planned the kill of Marty and did it. But he had ambitions and as long as I knew his part of the murder, I was in his way. Juries seldom convict a woman, you know. So it had to be either Buddy or me. One of us had to die and I didn't like to kill anyone myself . . . so I chose *you*, Mike. . . ."

"But . . . I . . . loved you, Helen."

"And now you have to die, Mike. I can't even let you have that few minutes to speak to the police when they come . . . and they will come, you know."

"I know."

The knife was in her hand . . . a long slim little thing that came close slowly. It came up closer . . . and I couldn't move out of the way at all.

"Mike . . . believe something. I really love you, Mike."

"I know, Helen. So now I die. But don't count on living too long, Helen. Someplace we might meet again . . . no matter where it is, you'll die, too, Helen."

"It will never happen that way, Mike." She sighed. "Mike . . . I'm sorry."

She thrust the blade.

46

The Night I Died

★ ★ ★ ★ ★

Die? Yeah, that was the night I died. It wasn't my skin and bones. No, my flesh had to live even though I didn't want it to.

But something else had died that night. Something more important than what you see when you look in the mirror.

My thumb found the hammer and pulled it back.

"Really here . . . Mike?"

"Really here, Helen."

"Not even a kiss good-bye, Mike?"

"Not even a kiss good-bye. The last one was two years ago. That one will hold me. That was a real kiss. A kiss of death. Remember it, Helen?"

Sure, she remembered it, all right. She came closer, with her arms reaching out for me and I wasn't supposed to see that same sliver of steel that she had used before.

"I really love you, Mike."

"And I really love you, Helen."

And then the only sound you hear is the gunshot, and her cry. And the sound of your own feet, walking down the street at night.

I'll Die Tomorrow

The friendly-looking gentleman in the neat charcoal grey suit was a killer. But like any good predator, his disguise was excellent. To all appearances, he was a moderately successful businessman with offices, perhaps, high in a Manhattan building, where the street fumes and noises didn't reach.

Offhand, you would guess his age in the late forties, and if asked to describe him, could do little more than say he was, well, average. No, there was nothing suspicious in his walk or talk or behavior and if you had any reason to trust anyone it would be this gentleman. Why, he even looked happy.

And with all of that, his disguise *was* perfect, simply because it was not an artificial disguise at all. It was real. He did have an office, although not in Manhattan, and he was happy. Rudolph Less was a man well satisfied with life, especially when he was working, and now he was on a job again.

Upstairs was a man he was going to kill and the going price on his demise was to be 10,000 lovely dollars that would go toward supporting his single secret pastime in his converted summer house on the Island. He smiled at the thought, feeling a tiny, vicarious thrill touch his parts. Women, he thought, could be taught . . . or even forced . . . to do such wonderful things.

Yes, life was fine. Only the select few knew of his true nature and of his niche in life. Through these few, others could come by his services—and many had.

How many now? Was it 46 times? Or 48? Sometimes it was difficult to recall. Once he had kept track, but as in all other businesses, tabulating inventory became boring. Now it was better simply to look ahead.

It was a good business and of all those engaged in it, he was the best. No doubt of it. (He smiled at the doorman who smiled back, but the smile was only a gesture.) He was thinking of the many times he had read the accounts in the papers of his work. Always, the police were puzzled, or another was taken in custody. He chuckled when he thought of the three who had already died in the chair mistakenly. Wouldn't *that* shake up the administration if it ever came out! But they were only punks and the error of their death was really a boon to society, doing earlier what would have happened later anyway.

Things like that only added to his business reputation, though. It had paid off, really it had. He thought again of Theresa of the dark flesh and darker hair who had loved those things he had done to her. She really had. She had done things to him that in his frenzy of wild emotion he couldn't even recall. He could only remember the terrible pleasure of the experience. Well, he could get Theresa again now.

That's what being the best meant. They hired him because he never failed. For a brief second his face clouded as if he were angry with himself, then he shook his head dismissing the thought because it couldn't be.

It was too bad, he thought, that he hadn't checked further, but experience wasn't on his side then. He had cleared out too soon. He wasn't absolutely certain. He smiled again, tentatively. But they had paid him, so everything must have gone all right.

49

He couldn't help but think about it and try to recall the details merely to satisfy his desire for perfection. It had been his first contract, and a simple one. A kid called Buddy . . . he couldn't remember his last name, but he had a dime-size hole through his right ear that was supposed to be from a stray .45 bullet during the war. Buddy had hijacked seventeen grand from the paymaster to the Jersey City group and rather than remain a laughing stock to their pseudo-dignity, Buddy had to go, but with no apparent connection to the group, of course.

It hadn't been difficult. Buddy was a talkative guy so he simply engaged him in conversation, walked him close to the water, enjoyed the final moment of conversation by telling Buddy who he was and what he was about to do and while Buddy stood dumfounded, with his mouth open and a light from the opposite shore visible through the hole in his ear, he chest-shot him and watched the body smash back into the water.

If only they had found the remains he could be satisfied. However, the river was running fast, it *had* been blowing up a storm, and the ocean was close by. Buddy (what *was* his last name?) never showed up, not even to reclaim the bundle of money he had left behind in his room. At the thought Rudolph Less breathed deeply and smiled, satisfied that his record was perfect. Yes, a good record. Big Tim Sheely of Detroit and the western Senator and Marco Leppert who was a Mafia courier were on that list. He chuckled again. How the Mafia had searched for him! They killed four men thinking they had the right one each time and he was never even suspected. After their last failure it was the Mafia itself who gave him the job of axman to rid the organization of their own killers who blundered.

That job got him Joan, he remembered. Such a woman,

such a hungry, hungry woman. She was so big all over. So big, so big. Everything so big. Yes, he would have Joan again too. Perhaps even Theresa and Joan together. Who knew what he could do then. It might be bad for his constitution, but he was in good health yet, he thought wryly. There were still some things to be experienced that he could stand.

He had no need to look at the wall directory before going into the elevator. He was part of the crowd now, seen, yet unnoticed. He coughed gently from the smoke of the cigar in the mouth of the man next to him but said nothing. Instead, he thought suddenly, *I'd like to kill him!*

Like Lew Smith who stood right in front of him in the back of the darkened theatre and never felt the ice pick slide into his heart. He simply collapsed and they carried him out thinking that he had fainted, and no one saw Rudolph leave at all. Lew smelled of cigar smoke too. And Lew had bought him Francie who would make him sit back and watch while she did the damnedest dance he ever did see until his eyes were bugging out and he could hardly breathe and when by the time she let him get his hands on her he had lost almost all his senses and had to be slapped back to normal. But Francie had smiled then and loved what he had done to her although she pouted a while over his bite marks.

He was breathing too heavily, and down the neck of the woman in front of him. She almost turned around, when he caught himself and forced his breath to come easier.

It was because he was getting close to his business arrangement again. It was like that lately. He tasted the fruits of success before the actual planting. But the conclusion was foregone anyway. Success was not problematical any longer. It was a certainty. That was why he could ask for so much to do so little.

Sometimes he wondered about those who lingered a few

moments. What did they think? Who was he? What had they
done to him that he should snuff out their lives? Oh, there
were those who knew. He remembered that two even seemed
relieved. For years they had lived in fear of this day and now it
had come. There was no more fear for them. Actuality had
arrived as a medium-sized man with a friendly smile and it
was over very quickly without much pain at all because he was
an expert at his work. He was quite sure that one man even
whispered a quiet "Thank you" before he died.

Well, that was one thing about his method. There was no
flight involved, no loud histrionics. They didn't know him,
there was nothing fearful about his appearance and if anything registered at all, generally it was surprise.

Someday, maybe, he thought he might like to change his
method. If he could get his assignment in the proper place he
would like to try a few experiments. Like extensions of the
things he had done with Lulu who had some savage blood and
liked to be beaten in certain ways. Pain peculiarly inflicted
with her fullest cooperation was her delight and she had
taught him things his mind had begun to dwell on lately. He
shrugged off the thought impatiently and looked up at the indicator over the operator's head. The car had stopped and the
doors opened.

Sixteen.

He remembered *his* number 16.

She was a showgirl named Cindy Valentine who knew too
much about the operations of another group through an already dead boyfriend. The District Attorney had her secretly
marked for investigation, but money, being able to buy anything, bought the tip and now Cindy was being canceled out.

Cindy Valentine, number 16, had been somewhat of a
pleasure. In fact, it had been Cindy who had showed him the
ultimate use to which he could put the many dollars he had

accumulated. So far he merely rented an office from which he sold, and profitably, trinkets and novelties via pages of certain magazines. One employee really did all the work but it gave him a sense of well being, a place in society. Daily, he commuted from his house. It wasn't much, but it was secluded. There was nothing he couldn't do there at his pleasure and he was so situated that there were no prying eyes at all. To the world outside, he lived a simple and secluded life. Sort of a friendly recluse, he thought.

Yes, Cindy had brought new meaning into his life. He had called ahead and said he was a jeweler who was instructed to let Miss Valentine have a single pick from his collection. She had been overjoyed at the thought and although she tried to cajole the name of his sponsor from him, he said he was sworn not to tell. Hers was a secret admirer. No doubt she had had many. She believed everything he told her. She squealed with delight when she admitted him to her apartment, seeing the flat sample case under his arm.

At first she didn't notice the flush in his face. She was too excited, then, in the living room, she saw his consternation and smiled. The filmy nylon negligee was all Cindy had on. Her smile grew impish and she had said, "Since you're going to give me something, I'm going to give you something." Then she let the negligee fall to the floor and when she was done he was a shaken but strangely elated man. She said, "Now you give me something," and looked at the case on the table. Well, he gave her something, all right. Very quickly and there was hardly any blood and he picked up his case and went out. They all called it a passion kill and in a way it had been.

Cindy certainly had introduced something new to his life. Now, rather than merely having the satisfaction of a job well done, he had an end result that was far greater than anything he had ever dreamed of. The satisfaction he would get tonight would be far greater than the satisfaction of job perfection he used to consider enough. Perfection was quite a word. It gnawed at him like a little mouse. If only he could have been sure of that first one. Buddy, the one with the hole in his ear.

Well, the one upstairs would merely add to his list of accomplishments. This was a curious one. Different insofar as he never had time to study the man. He would be alone in his office counting the weekly take, a secret office he used solely for bookkeeping and accounting purposes. He rented it under an assumed name and made a deliberate point to go there disguised. His operation was illegal and deftly concealed. Only after long and arduous investigation did Rudolph Less's client discover his whereabouts. Since his connection with the dead man would be obvious, it was necessary for his client to have an airtight alibi at the time of the kill, making Rudolph's talents necessary.

Ordinarily he wouldn't have gone for the second part of the arrangement, but lately he was beginning to enjoy new facets of an old thrill. The client said he could keep whatever money he found there in addition to his regular pay. Thousands extra! Enough to buy . . . well, if that man was right about that one down in Cuba he could bring her here at once. Complete muscular control, he had said. Think of it! He swallowed hard and dimmed the mental picture. Not yet. Later he could sit in his room savoring the anticipation when the job was done, but first the job.

He got out at 20 with two others but before the doors shut a giddy young girl ran up and grabbed his sleeve and said too loudly, "Mr. Brisson? Are you Mr. Brisson . . . they just called from downstairs and said . . ."

"I'm not Mr. Brisson," he smiled. Inwardly he swore, something he hadn't done in years. He saw the elevator boy grinning at the girl's stammer of embarrassment before the doors closed. An incident like that could cause that boy to remember his face. But nevertheless, he'd never be back again, never see the boy again, and if he described anyone at all, or did the girl, it would be the average man of the street.

The girl walked off, her buttocks in violent motion. Ordinarily he would feel a warm glow at such a sight, but the momentary pleasure of another sort ahead that could be completely consummated overrode such a simple delight of watching a girl from behind.

Yet the sight introduced a new thought, something that had been on his mind for months now, something that touched him whenever he saw a young and pretty girl on the street. So far he had bought his pleasures. Oh, they had been expensive, but worth every bit of it. But the thrills and sensations they provided finally reached a limit. Repetition turned original wonders into almost commonplace boredom and it was getting more difficult all the time to find something *really* different.

There *was* one thing. Supposing, and it shouldn't be difficult, that he could lure some unsuspecting girl . . . on the promise of a job, perhaps . . . or really, if one was honest about it, by actual force . . . that would take a car, maybe drugs; there would be untold risks but that would only add to the delicacy . . . yes, it was something to think about. Maybe after the one from Cuba. He would like to experience one with complete muscular control first.

Annoyed at himself he stopped and adjusted his coat, although there was no one in the corridor to see him. He held the leather folio more securely under his arm, feeling in it the flat contours of the Browning and the extended length of the silencer he had gotten from that odd man in Germany. Silencers were fine. Why didn't they fight wars with silencers? It

shouldn't be expensive and think of how quietly and effi-
ciently the war could be fought. Ah, the advantage of the bow
and arrow. Too bad it was such a clumsy weapon.

He stopped at the door marked *STAR DISTRIBUTING*,
smiled to himself and fitted the key he had been given into the
lock. It opened easily and he stepped inside. As the diagram
showed, he was in a small anteroom, and facing him was the
lighted square of a frosted glass door. That had no lock.
Rudolph Less smiled again.

He heard someone cough and nodded to himself. Feet
shuffled and a chair scraped back. He heard a phone picked
up and dialed and held his position. He could not enter while
the phone was on. There was no need for someone else giving
an alarm. The way it was, if done right, the body wouldn't be
found until it started to stink and that would be several days.
No, he could wait a minute.

Inside, his assignment said, "You got everything ready for
tonight . . . yeah . . . yeah . . . okay, I'll call you. I'm going to
make up the payroll now. Sure . . . sure . . . so long." The
phone clicked and the man coughed again.

Rudolph said softly, "Now," and opened the door.

He smiled at his assignment.

His assignment looked startled, then frowned uncompre-
hendingly at the Browning with the silencer pointing at his
chest. He was a big man, thick through the chest and neck, his
hair grey at the sides. He was well dressed and from first
glance Rudolph wouldn't have taken him for someone in the
rackets. But appearances were deceiving, weren't they? Who
would take *him* for an *eliminator?* Now that was a good word.

The man said, "What do you want?"

Rudolph's eyes took him in quickly. He was big, all right.
Most likely it would take more than one shot. Two quick
body hits to stop him if he tried to move, then a head shot to

complete the job. One thing about a silencer, you could hear the bullets hit too. Not so much in the stomach, of course, but if they went through a rib or in the skull . . .

"What I want is your money," Rudolph said. It sounded peculiar to him. Shoddy, somehow. "Where is it?"

"In the safe, that's where, and if you expect . . ."

"If I don't get it I'll kill you anyway," Rudolph told him.

There was no mistaking the tone of his voice. The big guy nodded, was about to say something and stopped. He walked across the room to the safe and dragged out a small, obviously heavy, steel box. Rudolph saw the combination lock on it and waved the gun to the desk. He surely couldn't carry the box out of here. "Open it," he said.

The guy sat down and began spinning the dial. Outside there was a burst of laughter and a key rattled the lock. The door opened and two girls laughed again. A male voice joined theirs.

Rudolph's heart jumped, but then quieted. He had been in situations like this before. He put the gun into the folio, keeping his hand on it and casually sat down. The door to the office opened and a girl said, "Mr. Riley, your friend Mr. Brisson is here. Do you want . . ." She glanced around the door and saw Rudolph. "Oh," she giggled, "I'm sorry. I didn't know you had company. I thought this man was Mr. Brisson before."

"That's all right," Mr. Riley told her. "I'll be out shortly."

The girl giggled again and closed the door. Outside several more people came in and typewriters began to rattle. Two men were discussing a sales meeting.

Rudolph could feel the dryness of his skin, but still he could smell sweat. Sweat? Or was it fear? Someplace something had gone wrong. This was supposed to be an empty office. Just one man. Damn! Why didn't he do the job the way

57

he had done all the others. That's what happens when you leave the details up to somebody else. Damn it all to hell! But you wouldn't know that was what Rudolph Less was thinking because he was smiling in a very friendly fashion.

The big man said softly, "You're in trouble, friend," and as he said it opened the lid of the box. The money was there as it was supposed to be. Packets of hundreds and Riley was dumping it out on the desk. He looked across the room at his smiling visitor. "You can't get out very well and pretty soon somebody will be coming in here. If you do get out you won't be a hard one to identify. Those girls out there are all artists and could sketch you to perfection. Show it to the papers and you'd be turned in in no time."

"That is problematical," Rudolph said.

"You picked a lousy time for a stickup, mister."

Rudolph smiled again. "Yes, I did." The smile didn't last long because Riley was smiling too.

He said, "Buddy, if I could get the jump on you, you'd be in a mess."

"Oh?" His teeth flashed and he lifted the Browning out of the folio.

"You had a key to this place, you came on a day when the payroll was being made up and you came armed. A planned stickup. I kill you . . ." he shrugged . . . "one day in court is all. Self defense."

"That could hardly happen," Rudolph said. For some reason he felt edgy. Events weren't at all like they should be. His assignment, a better word than victim, was being too aggressive. What had to be done had to be done quickly and his mind raced over the possibilities. Several were available to him. He would take the money, of course. He would tell them outside that Mr. Riley would be busy all day and not to disturb him. He'd hate to leave his house, especially his paraphernalia he had so carefully assembled, but he lived there under a fictitious name and he could do it over again, perhaps this time with certain innovations he desired. Suntan, hair dye, whiskers in any number of combinations could alter his appearance sufficiently. No it wouldn't be an insurmountable problem at all.

He was so engrossed in his thoughts, that although his eyes were on Riley, the big man's voice came to him as a steady drone.

". . . it took so long to find you. You're mighty clever, I guess you know. Proof for a court of law would be impossible to obtain. And me, I don't want to stick my neck out. I'm not going to kill somebody who needs killing bad then pay for it myself. I'm a little on the smart side too.

"But contacts I made. Finally the right guy put me through. In returning a big favor I did him he put me in touch with you. We made the arrangements together, you and I. Clever, eh?"

The big guy smiled and sucked in his breath. He was too big, Rudolph thought. Maybe even two chest hits wouldn't do it. He carried five in the Browning so what he'd have to do was give him four in the chest quickly and then hold the last one for the coup. Nobody could take four. The smashing impact in the lungs even prevents a yell and the only sound would be the body falling. However, the noise outside would cover that up.

Somehow the droning voice made sense. His mind, charged now to frenzied activity, raced back over the words, picked them up and went over them again. There was something here now that shouldn't be at all. Something terrible if he heard right. The smile seemed frozen on his face now and for the first time his eyes made a little rat's movement around the room.

"I hired you to kill me," Riley said. "I never knew who you were or where you were and I finally figured out the only way to have you in front of me so you could die where I can see it happen without any heat coming my way at all."

Rudolph's voice was strained. "You can't!"

"I have, pal, I have. But first let me tell you thanks. I have a nice straight business going for me and there won't be any heat. In fact, I'll be a hero. How about that."

He felt cold. He had never felt so cold as now. There was no spit in his mouth and his insides were rolling. Had he eaten earlier he was sure he would have vomited at that moment. For some reason he could hear the voices of Cindy and Lulu and Francie and Joan and all those others and far away mocking him with a Cuban accent the untasted one he hungered after, and somewhere from a deep invisible fog came the scared bleatings of the ones he would have had by cajolery or by force if necessary.

Would have had! Not at all! Not at all, Mr. Riley. "You forgot something, Mr. Riley," Rudolph said, bringing the Browning into line with his chest. "I have the gun."

"And I have one in this box under my hand, friend. A big fat .45 automatic for which I have a license."

Rudolph nodded sagely. "The moment you move your hand toward it I'll shoot you," he said softly.

"Fair enough," Riley said.

Rudolph was on his feet. What was the matter with this man? Was he mad! Then his hand moved and Rudolph pulled the trigger. The Browning jumped once . . . twice . . . three times . . . four . . . he could see the shots hitting his chest right in the heart area. Go down, damn you, go down! He had to go down. The big guy had the .45 out of the box when Rudolph Less pulled the trigger on the last shot and saw it rip into his arm, but it was the wrong arm. The other one had the .45.

And he was grinning, damn him!

He looked at the blood pumping from his arm. "This makes it all the better," he said, then laughed again and ripped open his shirt.

With mouth agape, Rudolph saw the overlapping plates of the bulletproof vest. Riley brought the gun up and pointed it at his head.

Rudolph was old looking now, sallow, his cheeks sunken in fear. His invincibility shattered for no reason, no reason at all. All those wonderful pleasures gone, gone, because this big fool in front of him had tricked him. Where had he made his mistake? It had to be somewhere. Where then?

He said, "Why?" His voice was weak, faltering.

Riley lifted a hand to his ear and felt for the piece of cosmetic wax that fitted so cleverly. Then he squeezed the trigger of the .45.

In the awful blast of the gun that Rudolph could still hear while his skull was shattering into tiny bits his last remembrance was that the round hole in the nose of his final lover, the terrible .45, was exactly the same size as the one in the big guy's ear and that Riley's first name had to be Buddy.

The Veiled Woman

Lodi's soft warm hand shook me awake. "Sh-h-h, Karl. Don't say anything." I could barely hear her. "There's someone down-stairs."

The .45 I kept under my pillow was in my hand before I had my eyes fully open. The bedroom was in total darkness because of the heavy curtains covering the windows, and the only sound was the almost inaudible purr of the air-conditioning unit. I pressed the fingers of my free hand lightly to Lodi's lips to still her whisper and to let her know I was now fully awake.

I swung my bare feet to the floor and stood up. The fact that I was as naked as one of Mike Angelo's cherubs didn't occur to me then, and even if it had I wouldn't have wasted time looking for a robe.

Moving on tiptoe, I crossed the room and was careful about shooting the bolts on the door. I could hear nothing from downstairs, but that didn't mean no one was down there. Lodi's almost incredibly sharp sense of hearing was something I had learned long ago not to doubt. Twenty years among the perils of the jungle develops the senses like nothing else, and the African jungle was where Lodi had come from.

With the door opened wide enough for me to slip through, I stepped into the upper hall. Still no sound. A tomb would have been noisier. No light either. It was like walking through a bottle of ink.

Still no sound from below. I wasn't surprised. Whoever was down there wouldn't be a common garden-variety burglar. Burglars didn't come out here in the wilderness eighty-odd miles north of New York City in search of loot.

I went down that flight of carpeted steps, like a jungle cat stalking its prey. The damp chill of early morning began to flow across my skin, reminding me of my lack of clothing. At the foot of the stairs I froze in my tracks, listening, making sure the safety catch on the .45 was off.

More silence. Nothing stirred, nothing breathed. Had Lodi been mistaken after all? Had her nerves, under a growing strain for almost two months now, finally started to give way? I refused to believe it. . . .

And then I heard it. A sound so slight that only keen ears straining to listen would possibly have caught it. The chink of metal against metal, and that only once.

The study. The wall safe was in there; a vault actually, built by the previous owner. It would be the natural place for an intruder to start his search.

Silently I crossed to the study door, the gun ready in my fist. The door, I discovered, had been left open no more than an inch or two to enable the man in there to catch any sound from outside the room.

Slowly, with almost painful care, I pushed the door inward. As the space between its edge and the jamb widened, I saw a circle of light fixed on the combination knob of the vault. A man was standing there, one ear pressed to the metal surface of the vault door, his fingers slowly manipulating the dial. He was alone.

63

I leaned forward and groped along the wall until my fingers found the light switch. I flipped it, flooding the room with light, said, "Cheerio, you son of a bitch," and shot him through the head.

The sound of the heavy .45 was like an exploding bomb in the confines of that small room. Blood and brains and bone showered the vault door and the black-clad figure melted into the rug.

"Karl!" It was Lodi calling from the head of the stairs. "Darling, are you all right?"

"I'm fine," I said. "Go on back to bed, baby. I'll be up in a minute."

"Did you . . . did you—?"

"I sure as hell did. I'll tell you about it over grapefruit in the morning."

I crossed the room and knelt beside the body. There wasn't much left of him above the eyebrows, and what was below them was a face I had never seen before. The pockets held nothing personal that might identify him. An oiled-silk packet containing as nice a set of burglar tools as you'd find anywhere, but that and a half-empty pack of Philip Morris made up the total.

I didn't like that. In fact, I liked it so little that I scooped the .45 off the rug and stood up, all in one quick movement.

Too late! Before I could turn around a silken drawl said, "No further, Mr. Terris. Stand perfectly still."

I said a couple words under my breath but that was as far as I went. I heard the rustle of silk and the sound of light steps coming toward my back. "Let the gun drop. . . . Now, kick it away from you."

I could smell her now: the music of an expensive perfume and the nice female smell of a lovely woman. The drawl said, "You may turn around now and lower your hands. Any more than that and I'll shoot you through the knee."

She was wearing black, broken only by a white appliquéd design just above the left breast. A pastel mink jacket hung casually from perfect shoulders and she was as blonde as a wheat field. It would have been a shame for her not to be beautiful, and beautiful she was, and not with the standard, nightclub kind of beauty that's almost commonplace these days.

"Which knee?" I said.

"I know all about you, Mr. Terris," she said coolly. "Forty million dollars and a sense of humor. Only I don't want any of either."

"That's a relief," I said. "What *do* you want?"

She was standing in front of me, a gun large in her hand, a slight smile tugging at the corners of an almost sensual mouth. Her eyes went over me frankly and with something more than faint approval. "Do you find the evening oppressively warm?"

I glanced down at my naked body, then back up at her. "I'm sorry. Would you like to wait while I run up and get into my dress suit?"

"I'm afraid we can't spare the time." She walked over to a lamp table and whisked the large scarf off it and tossed it to me. "Do something with this," she said. "I find your—well, your masculinity a little overpowering."

The scarf was on the skimpy side but I made it do. She leaned against the back of a lounge chair and went on pointing the gun at me. "And now back to business, Mr. Terris. I came here for that machine you brought back from Africa."

"You're not strong enough to lift it."

"Are you?"

"Just barely."

"That's fine. My car is waiting. You can carry it out and put it in the trunk."

I shook my head. "No dice, Blondie."

"You'd rather have a bullet through your leg?"

"Any day," I said. "Because some day the leg would heal, the bone would mend. And then I'd find you and I'd kill you. Nice and slow, then use your guts for shoe laces and your spine for a necktie rack."

She smiled. "Tough guy. We know all about you. I don't scare, Mr. Terris, but neither do you, unfortunately. Threatening you with personal injury is a waste of time. I told them that, but they wanted me to try it anyway. Well, I tried."

Without taking her eyes off me, she raised her voice. "Stephan. Gregory. Come here."

Two men, one large and bullnecked and with a face like a dropped melon, the other slim and white-faced and black-eyed, appeared in the doorway behind her. Both held guns in their right hands.

"Mr. Terris refuses to frighten, gentlemen," the girl said. "Go up and get Mrs. Terris. Tie and gag her and put her in the car. Let me know when you're ready to leave."

They turned silently and started out. I said, "Hold it." They kept on going. I said, "Call off your dogs, Sadie."

Her quiet voice stopped them as though they'd run into a wall. Her confident smile revealed flawless teeth. "Yes, Mr. Terris?"

"There is no machine. There never was."

Her smile now was almost sad. "Lies won't help. In fact, I'm surprised you even bother to try them on me."

"I mean it, Sadie. The first time I heard about my having a machine was ten days ago. Two men broke into my apartment in New York and demanded I hand 'the machine' over to them. You may have read about it in the papers."

The gun in her hand stayed as steady as Mount Hood. "Yes. You killed them both. With your bare hands, I believe—or was that just tabloid talk?"

"No."

"They were bunglers, Mr. Terris. I am not. Do you give us what we came for, or do we take your wife instead?"

My muscles began to ache from the strain of not jumping straight into the muzzle of her gun. "I'm telling you, Sadie: there is no machine. Somebody's given you a bum steer."

Her sigh was small but unmistakable. "Fifty-three days ago," she said, "you arrived in New York aboard a small steamer which you chartered at Dakar. This was almost exactly two years after your small plane crashed somewhere in the interior of French Equatorial Africa while you were searching for a uranium deposit in that section of the continent. Your government combed the area for weeks without finding any trace of your plane, and you were given up for lost. Am I correct so far?"

"The newspapers carried the story," I said.

"Your arrival in New York," she went on in the same even, unhurried voice, "created a major sensation. The country's richest, handsomest, most eligible bachelor had returned from the dead! Only the bachelor part no longer applied: you had brought back as your bride the world's most beautiful woman. I believe that's how she was described—although no one has been able to see her face clearly through the heavy veil she constantly wears. In fact, no one but you knows what your wife looks like. True, Mr. Terris?"

I shrugged and said nothing.

"You then placed your bride in the penthouse suite of a building you owned in Manhattan. You engaged no servants; you had no callers. No one—I repeat, *no one*—was permitted to enter your apartment. You were called to Washington to report on the success of your search for the uranium deposit. You stated that your mission was a failure. As a loyal and patriotic citizen as well as one of the wealthiest your statement was accepted and the matter closed."

She paused to raise an eyebrow at me meaningly. "Closed, that is, until two weeks ago. For it was about that time that a man and his wife were found dead in a small hotel in Nice. The cause of death was so startling that an immediate investigation was made. Do you know what killed those two people, Mr. Terris?"

"Measles?" I hazarded.

Her jaw hardened. "Radiation, Mr. Terris. A kind of radiation sickness not known before. Those two people died of cosmic radiation!"

"Do tell!"

She took a slow breath and her eyes bored into me. "Further investigation established that the dead couple had been exposed to the radiation roughly five weeks earlier. At that time they were occupying a cabin on a small steamer en route to Sweden. By a strange coincidence, Mr. Terris, it was the same steamer that brought you and your wife to America a few days before. By an even stranger coincidence, they had occupied the same cabin used by you and your wife. But the ultimate in coincidences, Mr. Terris, is that you had been in Africa in search of a fissionable material!"

"As you've pointed out," I said, "a matter of coincidence."

She shook her head. "I'm afraid it's not that simple. The inescapable conclusion is that, while in Africa, you discovered some method of trapping and converting the power of cosmic radiation. Either you found some natural substance that would do this, or—more likely—you were able to construct a machine that would do so. The residue from some leakage in the machine's operation was picked up by the unfortunate couple who next engaged that cabin, causing their deaths."

"No machine," I said. " I don't know what you're talking about. Go ahead. Search the house. But tell your goons to keep their hands off my wife. I mean it."

She wasn't listening. "Any country, Mr. Terris, who controls the secret you've learned will own the earth. As usual, your own government has only just learned the facts as I have given them to you. I happen to know that within a few days you'll be summoned to Washington and asked for the secret you hold. My government wants it instead—and we mean to have it!"

"If I had anything like what you're talking about," I said, "why wouldn't I have turned it over to Washington before this?"

She smiled. "I think I can answer that. It's well known that you are against war—that you narrowly escape being called a pacifist. To turn this secret over to the military of your government might very well lead to war."

"And in the hands of *your* government?"

"Peace, Mr. Terris. Peace because no other country or coalition of countries could prevail against us. Universal adherence to the principles of true democracy—the people's democracy."

"You mean communism, Sadie?"

"Exactly."

"Love that people's democracy," I said. "Slave labor, purges, secret police, rigged trials, mass executions. Goodbye, Sadie. Sorry, no machines today."

"You prefer that we take your wife?"

"A word of advice," I said. "Keep your nail polish off my wife. Otherwise I'll spend the rest of my life and forty million dollars, if it takes that long and that much, finding you and your stooges. And when I do, I'll be judge, jury and executioner. You'll die like no one ever died before."

My words were just words, but my tone and my expression were something else again. The color faded in her checks and the gun barrel wavered slightly. But her smile was steady enough and faintly mocking.

"I think you mean that," she said quietly. Her free hand moved up and settled the mink jacket closer about her flawless shoulders. "But I've learned long since to pay no attention to threats. . . . Last opportunity. Do you hand over what we came for?"

"You talk American real good, Sadie. They must have fine schools in Leningrad."

Her lips twitched. "Westchester, Mr. Terris. And one of the best finish—" She stopped abruptly and all expression faded from her lovely face. "Where is the machine?"

I spread my hands. "You're slipping your clutch, Blondie. No machine. I told you that."

Her patience began to break up. "You fool!" she blazed. "You're actually going to hand us your wife rather than surrender it? You're as cold-blooded as a snake, Mr. Terris!"

"You can call me Karl," I said.

She stepped back and nodded to the two men behind her. They came forward cautiously, guns ready, circled until they were behind me. I went on looking at the blonde, memorizing every line of her face, the lobes of her ears, the curve of her nostrils, the shape of her eyes. Suddenly the muzzle of a gun ground savagely into my back and a hand closed firmly on one of my naked arms. Before I could twist away the needle of a hypodermic lanced into my shoulder, the plunger thudded down and I staggered back.

I stood there panting, still staring at the girl. I could feel my lips curl back in a strained rictus of hatred. A buzzing sound began to crawl into my ears.

"It had better finish me, Sadie," I said around my thickening tongue. "If I come through this, you'll feed five generations of worms."

She was leaning slightly forward, her eyes glittering, the tip of her tongue touching her parted lips, her breathing quick and shallow, watching the drug take hold of me. The gun in her hand was forgotten.

I tried to lift an arm. Somebody had tied an anvil to it. The City Hall was glued to my feet. The room clouded, wavered, then slowly dissolved. I fell face forward into the ruins. . . .

II

A voice said, "You made two mistakes, Sadie. You let me see your face and you said too much. Just a little too much, but enough."

It was my voice. I was talking out loud, coming out of it. I opened my eyes and rolled over and looked at the ceiling. Back of my eyes somebody had built a fire and left the ashes.

After a while I tried getting to my feet. It seemed to take a long time, but I finally made it. I stood there holding onto the back of a chair and let my eyes move around the room.

Sunlight was fighting to get in through the half-closed Venetian blinds at the two windows. The man I had shot earlier was still dead on the floor, with a pool of almost black blood under what was left of his head. The vault door stood wide open with its contents scattered. The rest of the room had the look of being worked over by a platoon of Marines armed with bayonets. Upholstery had been ripped to shreds, pictures were torn from the walls, drapes were piled in one corner, bookcases had been cleared ruthlessly.

Anger began to rise inside me. I crossed to the ruins of the small bar in one corner of the room, found a bottle of bourbon and drank a solid slug of the contents. The stuff almost put me back on the floor, but when the first shock passed my brain was working again.

I went up the stairs at a wavering run. The bedroom door stood open and Lodi was gone. The room itself was as much a shambles as the study downstairs, and the rest of the house was no better.

"It's all right, Lodi," I muttered. "They won't dare harm you. They'll wait a couple of days for me to get good and worried, then they'll get in touch with me and try to make a deal. Only I'm not going to wait that long."

In the kitchen I ate toast and drank four cups of scalding black coffee. Then I went back into the study and picked up the phone and called a number in the Lenox Hill section of New York City.

"Eddie? Karl. Now get this. I want all yearbooks for the past ten years put out by all the finishing schools on the East Coast. Have them in your office two hours from now. . . . How the hell do I know? You've got an organization; put it to work. As fast as they come in put people to work going through them to pick out every girl who lived in Westchester County at the time she was attending school. The girl I want is around twenty-five or twenty-six, so tell them to keep that in mind. You've got two hours, and I don't want any excuses."

I slammed down the receiver while he was still talking and looked around for the gun I had dropped on the rug the night before. It was still there, half buried under papers from the vault. I went back upstairs to shave, bathe and dress, then found a shoulder holster for the .45 and slid my suit coat on over it.

I walked out the front door and down the driveway. It was getting on toward ten o'clock and the sun was hot on my shoulders. In the valley a mile down the slope was the nearest highway to New York. Cars and trucks moved along the concrete ribbon, looking like ants on a garden path.

My convertible was where I had left it the day before. I was checking the tires when the sound of an engine coming up the gravel road to the house froze me. I stepped behind the car and unbuttoned my coat and waited.

A grey Plymouth turned into the highway and stopped and a man in his early thirties got out from behind the wheel. There was no one else in the car. He saw me standing there, nodded and started toward me without hurrying. He wasn't anyone I knew.

When he was about twenty feet away I slid my hand under the left lapel of my jacket and said, "That's close enough, friend."

He stopped abruptly and stared at my right arm, a puzzled look on his smooth, not unhandsome face. "I'm afraid I don't understand this. Are you Mr. Terris?"

"That's right."

"I'd like a word with you."

"Sure," I said. "What word would you like?"

He smiled crookedly. "I wish you'd take your hand out of there, Mr. Terris. It gives me the feeling you're about to pull a gun on me."

"That," I said, "is the general idea. Just who the hell are you?"

He kept his hands carefully away from his body. "The name is Granger, Mr. Terris. I'm an agent with the Federal Bureau of Investigation. Would you like to see my credentials?"

"Not especially," I said. "What is it you want?"

He laughed shortly. "Well, to put it bluntly—you! It seems there's a Congressional committee meeting in Washington this afternoon and they want you there. The AEC, to be exact. I was asked to come up and—ah—escort you there."

I recalled that the blonde had said something about that a few hours earlier. Whatever her pipeline, it certainly was reliable. I shook my head. "Sorry, Mr. Granger. I won't be able to make it. Another engagement—a rather pressing one. Good-bye."

He wasn't smiling now. "Afraid you don't understand, sir. I have a subpoena calling for your appearance at that hearing."

"That's different," I said. I took my hand from under my coat and walked over to him. "Can I give you some breakfast before we leave?"

Granger eyed me warily. "No, thanks. I've had breakfast. We'd better be getting into New York. We're catching a twelve o'clock plane. I suppose you'll want to pack a bag."

"Good idea," I said and turned and started back to the house with him beside me. We went up on the porch and through the front door. Granger took one look at the wreckage from last night's activities and his jaw dropped. "What hap—"

That was as far as he got before the edge of my hand caught him sharply on the back of the neck. He folded like a carpenter's rule, out cold. I caught him before he hit the floor and carried him into the living room. I found some strong cord in the kitchen and bound his hands behind him and his feet to the legs of the couch, careful not to cut off the circulation.

He opened his eyes while I was finishing up. "You're making a serious mistake, Mr. Terris."

74

I tightened the last knot and straightened up. "You won't be too uncomfortable. Mrs. Morgan, the cleaning woman, should show up about two this afternoon and she'll cut you loose. Incidentally, you'll find a body in the study. My work; I'll tell you about it some day."

I was out the front door before he could protest further. The convertible came alive under my foot and I roared down the curving gravel side-road to where it joined the highway.

III

At eleven-thirty-six I pulled into the curb in front of an office building on Madison Avenue in the Seventies. I rode the elevator to the ninth floor and entered the first door to a suite that took up most of one corridor. The legend on that door read "Edward Treeglos, Investments." The only investment involved was the money I invested to keep the place staffed and functioning. I had set it up, under the management of Eddie Treeglos, a former college friend of mine, five years before, at the time I came into the vast holdings from my father's estate. Its purpose was to handle matters too confidential to be taken care of by the mammoth organization, further downtown, known as The Terris Foundation.

I passed the receptionist before she could get her nose out of a magazine, and charged into Eddie's private office without bothering to knock.

He was behind his desk, his sharp-featured intelligent face bent over a pile of thin, outsize volumes bound in everything from leather to glossy stock. He looked up as I came in.

"Did you know," he said, "that four out of every ten girls attending finishing school on the East Coast come from Westchester County?"

I said, "When I want percentages I'll ask for them. What have you got?"

He gestured toward the pile of volumes. "Help yourself, playboy. The pages with Westchester babes are marked, and I've got six girls in the other offices going through more books. If I never see a sweet innocent schoolgirl face again it'll be fine with me."

At one o'clock I was still going strong, flipping pages, scanning face after face, as many as thirty to a page. One of the office girls brought in sandwiches and coffee; they cooled and were finally taken away without my even noticing them.

Slowly my hopes were beginning to dim. Maybe that blonde was cleverer than I had supposed. Her seemingly careless remark might have been a deliberate plant to throw me off the track. If so, she was too good for her job; she should have been the head of the entire Russian M.V.B. And then, just when I was about ready to sweep the books to the floor with rage, I spotted the face I was hunting for.

I came close to missing it entirely. She wore her hair different then and her face was fuller. But the angle to her nose and the high cheekbones and the slope of her jaw were unmistakable. She stared up at me from the glossy paper, the eyes wide and direct, the same faint curl to her lips. *Do you find the evening oppressively warm, Mr. Terris?*

Under the photo were several lines of type. They told me her name was Ann Fullerton, that she lived at 327 Old Colony Drive, Larchmont, New York, that she was a political science major. She belonged to a swank sorority, was vice-president of her senior class and had been mixed up in a lot of campus activities that probably would make fascinating reading for her children—if she lived long enough to have any.

My eyes went back to the mocking smile. "Laugh, baby," I

muttered. "Laugh while you can. Your belly will make me a fine dart board."

Across the desk, Eddie stared at me open-mouthed. "Take it slow, pal. You sound like a goddamn tax collector."

I ripped the page out, shoved a pile of the books to the floor and pulled the phone over in front of me. "Tell the help to forget it. I've found what I'm after."

"Sure, sure. You feel like telling me what's going on?"

"Next week," I said. "You got a Westchester phone directory?"

He shrugged, reached out and flipped a lever on the intercom and told the receptionist to bring one in. I leafed through the Fullertons and found an Eric Fullerton living at the same address in Larchmont shown on the page from the yearbook. I dialed the number.

"Fullerton residence," a man's voice said.

I made my voice brisk and business-like. "Is this Mr. Fullerton?"

"Mr. Fullerton is not in, sir. Caldwell, the butler, speaking. Is there a message?"

"I'll talk to Ann Fullerton," I said.

The silence at the other end lasted long enough to be shocked. ". . . I'm afraid there's some mistake, sir. Miss Ann Fullerton died almost a year ago."

"*What!*"

"Yes, sir."

I got my chin up off my necktie. "Look—uh, Caldwell. Is Mrs. Fullerton there?"

"Yes, sir. Who shall I say is calling?"

"My name is . . . Carney. Alan Carney."

"One moment, Mr. Carney."

The receiver went down and I lit a cigarette, getting over the shock. There wasn't the slightest chance that the girl in the yearbook and the girl who had held a gun on me a few hours before were not one and the same. I had studied her face much too carefully to be mistaken.

A quiet voice said, "This is Mrs. Fullerton."

I said, "I hate to bother you, Mrs. Fullerton. I had no idea, of course, that your daughter . . ."

"I understand, Mr. Carney."

"You see, it's very important that I get in touch with a former friend of Ann's. A girl named . . . Taylor—Mollie Taylor. I wonder if you could tell me anything about her."

"I'm afraid not, Mr. Carney." Her voice sounded flat, almost weary. "You see, I didn't know Ann's friends. She hadn't lived with us for nearly two years before her death."

I said, "Would you mind giving me her address at the time? It's just possible somebody there could help me."

"We never knew her address, Mr. Carney. Ann was employed by an importing company. Anton & Porkov, I believe it was called."

"In New York?"

"Yes. I don't know the street address."

I wrote the name on a pad. "You've been very patient, Mrs. Fullerton. I know how painful all this has been for you. But would you mind telling me the circumstances of your daughter's death?"

There was a lengthy pause during which I expected her quietly to hang up the receiver. When she finally did speak I could barely hear her. "Ann died in a warehouse fire. I'm afraid that's all I can tell you. Good-bye, Mr. Carney."

A dry click told me the connection had been broken. I hung up and sat there staring at my thumb. All I had to do now was find a girl who had died months before, but who last night had engineered the kidnapping of my wife. Lodi's secret was now known to at least three people other than me. I should never have taken her out of Africa. I thought of her in the hands of those two silent ghouls and the blonde and a cold fury shook me. The mere fact that they had discovered what was behind Lodi's veil meant they must die. How they would die would depend on how they had treated her.

Eddie Treeglos was watching me wide-eyed. I tripped the lever on the intercom and said to the receptionist, "Get me the street address of Anton & Porkov, importers." I closed the key and leaned back in my chair and looked at Eddie through the smoke of my cigarette. "Does that name—Anton & Porkov—mean anything to you?"

"Can't say it does."

"My wife was snatched last night, Eddie."

"We'll get her back, Karl."

"Yes," I said. "Yes, we'll get her back." I got up and walked across the office and slapped my hand hard against the wall. For no reason. I turned and came back to the desk just as the intercom buzzer sounded. I moved the key again. "Well?"

"There is a listing for Anton & Porkov at 774 West Thirty-first Street, sir. The phone number is Clinton 9-5444. Also a listing for Sergi Porkov at 917 East Sixty-eighth. Butterfield 4-6793. It's the only other Porkov in the book, so it may be the same man."

I wrote it all down and closed the line. "I want a full report on that outfit, Eddie. They're importers; Washington should give you a line on them. No direct inquiries; I don't want them to know they're being checked. You've got half an hour."

"You're the boss."

"Yeah." I tossed the page from the yearbook across the desk to him. "Ann Fullerton. Check the police files to learn if she's got a record. Call Osborne at the FBI and see if he's got

79

anything on her. And anything else you think of."

"Right."

I moved my hand and the .45 was in it, pointed at him. All he did was blink. "Just finding out if I've still got the speed," I said.

He nodded. "I never even saw your hand move, brother."

"That's nice to know," I said. I picked up the slip with the addresses and phone numbers on it, folded it small and put it behind my display handkerchief. "I'll call you in half an hour. About Anton & Porkov."

"Okay."

I gave him a brief nod and walked over to the door and out.

IV

I stopped off at the Roosevelt Hotel and had lunch in the Men's Grill, then supplied myself with a handful of change and entered one of the phone booths. I put through a person-to-person call to Senator McGill at the Senate Building in Washington. My father had put him in office almost sixteen years before, and kept him there. When you own between forty and fifty million bucks in one form and another you need a loud voice where it can be heard.

His secretary told him who was calling and he came on the wire very excited. "Karl, you young idiot, are you trying to ruin me?"

"That's what I like about you, Senator," I said. "Always worrying about your friends rather than yourself."

"Oh, stop it! Have you any idea what the penalty is for attacking a Federal officer?"

"How did he work it so fast?" I asked. "I figured Mrs. Morgan would be untying him about now. What's behind all this subpoena business anyway?"

His voice was desperate. "You're in trouble, boy. The AEC says you lied about not getting anything useful out of Africa. They have good reason to think you came out of there with some kind of gadget to do with cosmic energy, whatever the hell that is. You better get down here and straighten things out before it's too late."

"Nuts to that," I said. "I got something a lot more important to take care of. Get them to call off their dogs."

His voice went up four octaves. "You think I'm the President? Not only does the AEC want you for questioning, but you're charged with attacking an FBI man and committing a murder! You grab a plane and get out here in nothing flat. Demarest of the Attorney General's office called me not more than half an hour ago and said they were getting out a general alarm to have you picked up."

"Get it canceled."

"I tell you I can't! What's more, they've issued a subpoena for your wife. Word's gotten around she's the one who gave you that gadget, and this business of her going around heavily veiled, no one ever seeing what she looks like, is beginning to look mighty suspicious."

"You think I give a damn how it looks? I'm telling you, get these alphabet boys out of my hair. Or are you tired of being a senator?"

"Don't you threaten me, you young upstart! I was making laws in this country while you were still soiling diapers. My record—"

"Stick your record," I cut in. "You get that general alarm withdrawn and those subpoenas held up or I'll plaster the darker side of your precious record over the front pages of every newspaper in the country."

He was still sputtering when I slammed down the receiver.

I went into the Rough Rider Room at the Roosevelt and had a couple of bourbons to settle my lunch and get the taste of politicians out of my mouth. My strapwatch showed 2:10. I went out into the hot sun and slid behind the wheel of the convertible and drove through a blue fog of exhaust fumes until I reached the 700 block on West Thirty-first.

It was a crummy neighborhood. Ancient loft buildings and sagging tenements and flyspecked delicatessens and cut-rate liquor stores and wise punks hanging around corner taverns. It stunk of dirt and poverty, with an occasional whiff of stale water and dead fish from the Hudson River a block to the west. A puff of tired air moved through the littered gutters and blew dust in my face.

I parked behind a truck half a block from 774 and waded through dirty-faced brats and sloppy-breasted housewives until I reached a corner drugstore. There were a couple of phone booths at the rear and I called Eddie Treeglos from one of them.

"What've you got, Eddie?"

"A thing or two. One, Sergi Porkov, alias Sam Parks, is one of the top Russian agents in this country. At present he is reported to be somewhere in Mexico. He's a tall blond guy, in his early forties, looks like a Swedish diplomat—at least that's the way my source of information described him—and has three rather large pockmarks on his left cheek. Two, Maurice Anton, his former partner in the importing firm, died of cancer at Morningside General Hospital four months ago. At that time Porkov sold the importing business to a man named Luke Ritter; no record on him but he's suspected of being a front man for Porkov. That's it, Karl."

I breathed in some of the booth's odor of cheap cigars. "Anything on Ann Fullerton?"

"Yeah. Identified by a close friend as one of the victims of

82

a fire nine months ago at a warehouse owned by the Fullbright Radio Company. Body was too badly burned for the parents to make a positive identification, but a purse under the body was hers. It was in the papers at the time."

"Who was the friend that made the ID?"

"Nobody seems to know. I'm working on it."

"Anything else on her?"

"Well, she was one of these college pinks. Carried banners on a couple of picket lines, belonged to several commie front outfits and so on. But right after she left school she dropped out of sight and nobody seems to have heard of her until she got too close to the fire. Except for one possible connection."

"Let's have it, Eddie."

"Here about eight, nine months ago, Sergi Porkov came up with a new girlfriend a knockout of a blonde named Arleen Farmer. The similarity in initials could mean something."

"You can bet on it," I said. "Got an address on her?"

"She was living with Porkov at the Sixty-eighth Street address."

"Nothing else?"

He sounded aggrieved. "My God, isn't that enough? You only gave me half an hour."

I cut him off, got out the list of addresses and phone numbers the girl at Eddie's had given me, and looked up Porkov's home phone. I stood there and listened to the buzz come back over the wire. No answer. I let it ring a dozen times before I decided that Anton & Porkov was the place to start.

I hung up and stopped at the cigar counter for cigarettes. Outside, the sun still baked the street. I walked slowly on down to 774, a loft building of battered red brick, four floors, with a hand laundry and a job printer flanking the entrance.

The lobby was narrow and had been swept out shortly before they built the Maginot Line. It smelled like toadstools in the rain, with a binder of soft-coal smoke held over from the previous winter.

A thin flat-faced kid with horn-rimmed glasses and a mop of black hair was propped up on a backless kitchen chair outside a freight elevator, buried to the eyebrows in a battered copy of Marx's *Das Kapital*. I brought him out of it by kicking one of the chair legs.

"Fie on you," I said. "You ought to know that stuff's rank bourgeois deviationism."

He looked up at me like a pained owl. He couldn't have been much past seventeen, if that. "I *beg* your pardon?"

"Now take Trotsky," I said. "There was a boy you could learn something from. Yes, sir. He had the right slant, that boy."

The kid's expression said he was smelling something stronger than toadstools. "Such as?" he snapped coldly.

"Search me. I'm a States Rights man myself." I indicated the cage. "How's about cranking this thing up to the fourth floor?"

He closed the book, leaving a finger in to mark his place. "Whom did you wish to see?"

"You figure on announcing me?"

He sighed, registering patience. "No, sir. That's the offices of Anton & Porkov. They're closed."

"This time of day? What will the stockholders say?"

He came close to saying what was on his mind, but changed it at the last moment. "Mr. Ritter hasn't come back from lunch yet."

"What about the rest of the help?"

"There is no one else, sir. Only Mr. Ritter."

"Certainly no way to run a business. Where does Luke have lunch? At Chambord's?"

"No, sir. At the Eagle Bar & Grill. Around the corner, on Twelfth Avenue."

I was turning away when he added: "And for your information, sir, Leon Trotsky was a counter-revolutionary, a tool of Wall Street, a reactionary and a jerk. Good afternoon."

I was halfway to Twelfth Avenue before I thought of an answer to that.

V

There was the smell of beer and steam-table cuisine, but not much light. I stepped inside and waited until my eyes adjusted to the dim interior. Four men were grouped at the bar discussing something with the man in the white apron, and further down the room another man in a crumpled seersucker suit sat at a small round table wolfing down a sandwich. A tired-looking blonde waitress was folding napkins in a booth at the rear of the room. I leaned across the bar and, during a sudden silence, beckoned to the apron. "I'm looking for Mr. Ritter."

A thumb indicated the man at the table. The silence continued while I walked back there and swung a chair around and sat down across from him. His head snapped up and I was looked at out of a pair of narrow dark eyes set in an uneven face that seemed mostly jaw.

"Mr. Ritter?"

". . . What about it?"

I said, "We can't talk here. Let's go up to your office."

He said, "Hah!" and bit into his sandwich and put what was left of it down on the plate and leaned back and chewed slowly, with a kind of circular motion. "What we got to talk about?"

"Not here," I said again. "You never know who's listening."

"I don't know you. What's your name?"

"My name wouldn't mean a thing to you, Mr. Ritter. Let's say I'm an old friend of Maurice Anton's."

His jaws ground to a halt and for a moment he seemed not to be breathing. Then he took a slow careful breath and his hands slid off the table and dropped to his knees. "Maurice, hunh?" he grunted. "Well, well. And how is Maurice these days?"

"He hasn't been getting around much," I said. "They buried him four months ago."

He went on staring at me without expression. The waitress got out of the booth and carried the folded napkins over to the bar. Ritter brought up a hand and picked up the heavy water glass beside his plate and emptied it down his throat. When he set it down again he kept his stubby fingers around it.

"Like I said, mister," he growled, "I don't know you. You got something to say, say it here. Otherwise, beat it."

I lifted an eyebrow. "That's no way to talk to a customer, Luke. Let's go up to your office."

"Customer, hell! You smell like a cop to me!"

There was no point in wasting any more time. I moved my hand and the .45 was in it, down low, the muzzle resting on the edge of the table and pointed at him. "Your office, Ritter," I said very quietly.

His whole body twitched spasmodically, then seemed to freeze. Behind me the voices went on at the bar. Ritter's eyes were glued to the gun and his heavy jaw sagged slightly.

"You can stand up now," I murmured. "Then you walk on out the door and straight to 774. I'll be riding in your hip pocket all the way; one wrong move and you'll have bullets for dessert. Get going!"

He wet his lips, still staring at the gun, and started to get up and an arm and a pair of female breasts came between us. That goddamn waitress.

She got as far as "Will that be—?" before Ritter grabbed her with one hand and threw the water glass at my head with the other. I ducked in time, but my gun was useless with the girl between us. Glass broke, somebody cursed, the blonde screamed and I moved.

I bent and grabbed Ritter's ankle and yanked. He fell straight back, taking the girl with him in a flurry of suntan stockings and white thighs. I tried shoving her aside to ram the .45 against Ritter's ribs, and he clawed out blindly, trying to hold her, caught the neckline of her apron and ripped it and the brassiere beneath completely away. This being July, she had dressed for comfort; and any lingering doubt over her being a true blonde was gone forever.

The blonde let out a screech that rattled the glassware and tried to get out from under. Somebody plowed into me from behind and I rammed against her, both of us crashing down on Ritter. I lost the .45 when my hand hit a chair leg, and a second later I was buried under an avalanche of humanity.

Fists, feet and knees banged into me from all angles. I managed to turn on my back and draw my knees up, then snapped my feet into the barman's belly, like the handsome hero of a Western, and threw him halfway across the room into a pinball machine.

It let me get to my feet. Ritter was running for the door, the blonde was trying to crawl under a table, giving me a view of her I would never forget, and facing me were the four guys I had first seen at the bar.

No sound but heavy breathing. The screen door banged behind Ritter. The barman began slowly to untangle himself from the ruins of the pinball machine, like a fly pulling loose from a sheet of Tanglefoot.

I said, "Get the hell out of my way," and walked straight at the four of them. The one in front of me looked plenty tough. He put up his fists in the standard boxing position and came up on the balls of his feet and took a couple of dancing steps toward me. I said, "You look a little pale to be Joe Louis," and slammed a hard right to his chin. He fell straight forward and I sidestepped and caught the next man by his belt and shirtfront and threw him into the pyramided bottles and mirror behind the bar. It sounded like Libby-Owens blowing up.

The remaining pair goggled at me and got out of the way. Not the barman, though. He took one look at the wreckage behind the bar, let out a bellow of rage and pain and charged me head-down. I stepped aside and put out my foot. He tripped and went sprawling into the booth where the blonde was crouched, landing squarely on top of her. I hoped they both would be very happy.

I scooped my gun off the floor and headed for the front door. Just as I got there a blue uniform pushed through a knot of spectators gathered outside and opened the screen. One of New York's finest—big and wide and handsome. He took one look at the gun in my fist and reached for his holster. I yelled and jumped forward and nailed him on the side of the jaw. The blow spun him in a limp circle and he fell halfway into an open phone booth. A few of the hardier members of the mob outside let out a yell and started to come in after me, but the sight of the gun melted them like snow in Death Valley. I realized, however, that leaving by the front door would be foolish at best, and more than likely ruinous. That left the back way, if there was one, and I headed in that direction.

A swinging door let me into a combination storeroom and kitchen, with a bolted door off that. I shot the bolts and opened the door and stuck my head out for a cautious look around. A narrow alley, crowded with torn papers, overflowing garbage cans and big fat blue-bottle flies buzzing in the hot sun. The stink would have taken top honors from a family of skunks, but it was nothing I couldn't live through.

Nobody in sight. I slid the gun back under my arm and trotted along the uneven bricks toward Eleventh Avenue, a block to the east, past loading platforms and the rear entrances to the buildings fronting on Thirty-first Street. Most of them had street numbers chalked up for the benefit of deliverymen, and my mind was already made up by the time I reached 774.

A sagging wooden door with four glass panels, three of them broken, the fourth coated with dust and cobwebs. There had been a lock on it once, but that was a long time ago. I peered through one of the broken panes. A dim and dusty corridor led toward the front of the building, with a closed door at the far end.

There was no time for advance planning. Any moment now cops would be pouring into the alleyway with blood in their eyes and guns in their hands. I pushed the door open, getting a complaining groan from rusty hinges, closed it carefully behind me and went quickly along the passageway to the inner door. I listened for a long moment, heard nothing but the faraway mumble of traffic; then turned the knob and gave it a small even tug. The door swung toward me an inch or two and I put an eye to the crack.

He was still there, no more than twenty feet away, in exactly the same position, still gulping down Marx and looking as though it agreed with him.

And between us, in the same wall as the elevator, was the entrance to the building stairs.

As a cause for rejoicing it left a good deal to be desired.

Getting to those stairs without the kid seeing me depended on just how strong a hold Marx had on him. Three or four steps would get me there, but the door had to be opened as well, not to mention the one I was standing behind. Of course, I could always shove my gun in his back, tie and gag him and dump him behind something, and use the elevator. But it would be a hell of a lot better to leave him undisturbed in case the cops came snooping around hunting for me.

I took another minute to study the kid's position. He was facing three quarters away from me, one shoulder propped against the wall, head bent over the book. To see me at all he would have to turn his head halfway around. No reason for him to turn his head unless I stumbled over my feet on the way.

It went off without a hitch. I was across the open stretch of hall and through the stairway door and had it closed again and my back against it within the space of six heartbeats. Now that it was over with, I had the feeling I could have driven an oil truck past the kid without his knowing it.

I climbed the three flights, found the door at the top unlocked and stepped into the hot dry air of a narrow hall with office doors, closed, lining both walls. None of the frosted glass panels had legends painted on them until I got down to the far end of the corridor. Three of the doors there, side by side, had the words "Anton & Porkov—Importers" painted on them in black, with the additional word "Entrance" on the one in the center.

I was standing there eyeing the center door and wondering if the thing to do was knock first, when a telephone suddenly shrilled behind the door on the left. I froze. A second ring broke off in the middle and the heavy voice of Luke Ritter said, "Yeah? . . . Not yet, no. . . . Any minute now. He was due in from Mexico City two hours ago. . . . I doubt it, Max. I called her but nobody answered. She probably met the plane. . . . I'll be right here."

The sound of a phone going back into its cradle. Some more silence behind the door. Then a chair creaked and another voice said, "That eye don't look any too good, Luke." It was a light, smooth voice, almost feminine.

"It hurts like hell," Ritter growled. "I'd like to get my hands on that bastard for about one minute. One minute's all I'd need!"

"You make him for a cop?"

"Naw. A cop would've pushed his badge at me. I figure him for a private dick trying to get a line on Porkov. He'll hear about it when he calls me."

"Any chance of the guy showing up here?"

A dry short laugh. "I sure as hell hope so, brother. The minute he walks into the lobby, the punk downstairs will ring our private buzzer. That's all the notice I want!"

I went on down to the third of the three doors marked Anton & Porkov and tried the knob. Locked. Nothing was easy for me today. This was an old door, fitting the frame loosely after many years. I reached in behind my display handkerchief and got out the nail file I carried there. It was thin enough for my purpose; I hoped it would be long enough. By pressing the knob hard away from the jamb I was able to slip the point of the file against the slope of the spring lock. It moved slightly, then snapped back with a light, almost inaudible, click. I opened the door. Nothing moved inside. I stepped through and closed it tenderly behind me.

It was a large square room, dim in the afternoon light filtering through a single unwashed window. Heavy wooden packing cases were stacked to the ceiling in two of the corners. A roll-top desk held a clutter of invoices, bills and loose papers. A communicating door was unlocked and I passed

91

through it into the center office. This one held metal files, a desk with a typewriter on the shelf, several chairs, a washstand behind a black lacquered screen in one corner. I could smell dust and, very faintly, a touch of cologne. Another door, closed, led to the first office, with the murmur of voices straining through it.

I went over to it, making sure my shadow wouldn't appear on the pebbled glass. The voices went on mumbling. The .45 came out, cool and comforting against my palm. I began a slow turning of the doorknob, the way they take the fuse out of a blockbuster. The door gave just enough to tell me what I wanted to know.

I slammed it all the way open with a hard movement of my knee and said, "Merry Christmas, you sons-a-bitches!"

That was as far as I got. Luke Ritter was behind a desk, tilted back in a swivel chair and looking at me with a twisted grin. He was alone. Even as I realized he couldn't be alone, something swished through the air behind me and the room exploded into a pain-filled void of stars. I felt myself falling as from a great height, then the stars were gone and nothing was left.

VI

Water trickled down my face and under my collar. I swam up from the depths into a pale green world of twisted shapes. Another wave of water poured over me and I sneezed suddenly, sending a lance of pain through my head.

I opened my eyes. I was flat on my back. Up above me floated a pair of pale balloons with grotesque faces painted on them. I blinked a time or two before my eyes focused, and then the balloons were faces after all. The familiar undershot jaw, slept-in features and dark eyes belonged to Luke Ritter; but the other was a pale cameo of delicate perfection, the face of a dreamer, a poet, a faerie prince. Eyes of azure blue widened appealingly, perfect lips parted to show beautiful teeth and a voice like muted viol strings said, "You want I should rough him up some more, Luke?"

"You did fine, Nekko," Ritter said. He drew back his foot and slammed his toe into my ribs. "All right, snoop. Up you go."

I rolled over and got both knees and one hand under me and tried to stand up. My head weighed a ton and was as tender as a ten-dollar steak. A hand came down and took hold of my hair and lifted me three feet in the air. The pain almost caused me to black out a second time. The edge of a chair hit me under the knees and I sat down, hard. The room moved around a time or two, then lurched to a stop. It looked only slightly better that way.

I could see my gun over on a corner of the desk, much too far away to reach by any sudden move on my part. Ritter gave me a cold smile and went around behind the desk and sat down in the swivel chair. He reached out, lifted the .45 by its trigger guard, swung it idly back and forth between thumb and forefinger and looked at me over it.

"You're kind of a secretive guy, mister," he grumbled. "I kind of went through your wallet while you were sleeping. Some money, but no identification. Just who the aching Jesus you supposed to be?"

"The name's Trotsky," I said. "My friends call me Cutie-pie."

Ritter stopped swinging the gun and lifted a corner of his lip. "Nekko," he said quietly.

A small hard fist came out of nowhere and hit me under the right eye. It hurt, but not enough to get excited about. I turned my head far enough to look at the beautiful young man called Nekko. I said, "Hello, honey. How're the boys down at the Turkish bath?"

His flawless complexion turned scarlet. He lashed out at me again but I moved my head quickly and he missed. He tried again, instantly, but his rage made him careless and he got too close to me. I lifted my foot hard and caught him squarely in the crotch. He screamed like a woman and fell over a chair.

Ritter bounded to his feet, came quickly around the desk and hit me high on the cheek with a straight left. No one had ever hit me harder in my life. My chair went over backwards with me in it. The back of my head hit the carpet and the light from the desk lamp blurred in my eyes. Ritter, his mouth twisting in a snarl, followed me down, trying to hit me again, this time with the gun. I took a glancing blow on the shoulder and grabbed the gun hand and tried to bite it off at the wrist. He slammed a fist into my throat and I vomited against the front of his shirt. That was when I got the barrel of the .45 behind my left ear and I went to sleep again. . . .

When I opened my eyes I was back in the same chair. Ritter was over behind the desk mopping his shirtfront with a wet handkerchief and swearing in a monotonous undertone that sounded like the buzz of a rattler. Nekko sat in a straight-backed chair tilted against the wall. His azure eyes stared at me with distilled hate through a veil of blue cigarette smoke. A good deal more important was the short-barreled .32 revolver he was holding against his thigh.

My head felt like a busted appendix and my throat wasn't any improvement. I sat there and caught up on my breathing and thought bitter thoughts. The room was ominously quiet.

Ritter finally threw the handkerchief savagely into a wastebasket and lifted his eyes to me. "Let's try it again," he snarled. "Give me your name."

"Take it," I said. "I can always get another."

"You come busting in here with a gun, smart guy. All I got to do is call in the cops and you end up behind bars."

"Ha ha," I said.

He stood up casually and came over to me and swung the back of his hand against my face. I rolled with the blow but that didn't help much. I tried to kick him in the shin but missed and it earned me another belt in the face. I felt my teeth cut into the inner surface of my cheek and the salt taste of blood filled my mouth.

Nekko slid out of his chair and jabbed the .32 against the back of my neck. Ritter bent down until his face was inches from mine. His breath was the reason they'd invented chlorophyll.

"Your name, you son of a bitch!"

I spat a mouthful of blood squarely into his eyes. He bellowed like a branded bull and swung a punch that started from the floor. Even though Nekko's gun was boring into my neck I jerked my head aside. The fist whistled past my ear and knocked Nekko's gun clear across the room.

It was my chance—maybe the last one I'd get. Before Ritter could recover his balance I slammed a shoulder into his gut and knocked him across the desk. Nekko was already across the room, bending to pick up the gun. I picked up the chair and threw it. It caught him in the ribs and spun him against a filing case. I jumped for the gun, snatched it up and turned, just as Nekko, his small white even teeth gleaming behind a crazed snarl, sprang at me. I took one step back and hammered the gun barrel full into his half-open mouth. He sprayed broken teeth like a fountain and his scream was half gurgle from the blood filling his mouth. He staggered back a few steps clutching his face, then collapsed into a sobbing heap.

95

I wheeled, just in time to see Ritter leveling my own gun at me from the opposite side of the desk. The look on his face told me he meant to blast me down and worry about the consequences afterward.

The .32 jumped in my hand with a spiteful *crack*. A red flower seemed to blossom under Ritter's left eye. The .45 dropped from his extended hand and bounced once on the blotter. Ritter turned in a slow half circle, took a wavering step going nowhere, then fell like the First National Bank.

I stood there, listening. Doors didn't slam, no feet came running down the hall, no one yelled for the police. Evidently the rest of the fourth floor was deserted, and from any place else that single shot could have been the slamming of a distant door or the filtered backfire from a car. The only sound was the bubbling sobs from the crumpled and no longer beautiful man known as Nekko.

I went behind the desk and looked at Ritter. He was as dead as Diogenes. I picked up the .45 and slipped it back under my arm and came back to where Nekko lay. Picking him up was like picking up a bucket of mush. I flopped him into a chair and took a handful of his wavy blond hair and shook him.

"Arleen Farmer," I said. "Where do I find her?"

His mouth dripped crimson like a fresh wound. The shattered stumps of teeth winked through the red. A vague mumble ground its way into the open. His eyes were completely mad.

I gave his head another shake. "Arleen Farmer," I said again. "Where is she?" I slapped him across the face and wiped the blood on his coat. "Talk, damn you!"

". . . do'n know . . ."

I hit him squarely in the nose. More blood spurted. His eyes rolled up and he fell off the chair. I kicked him full in the mouth. Even the stumps went this time. I tore off his necktie and bound his hands behind his back and left him lying there. My only hope was to find an address book that might give me additional leads to the kidnappers of my wife.

I stepped over what was left of Luke Ritter and started through the desk drawers. I was halfway through the junk in the center one when the phone rang.

VII

I stood there staring at the phone under the cone of light from the desk lamp. It rang a second time before I reached out and took up the receiver. "Yeah," I said, trying to pitch my voice to the same dull rumble I'd heard Ritter use.

A soft feminine drawl came over the wire. "Luke? Did Max call you?"

My fingers tightened against the hard rubber and my lips pulled back into an aching grimace. It was the voice of the blonde responsible for snatching my wife. I fought down a wave of pure fury and said, "Yeah. A while ago."

"All right," the soft voice went on. "When he calls back, tell him Sergi wants the woman brought to his apartment at ten o'clock tonight. Use the rear entrance and the service elevator. Got it?"

"Yeah."

"That's all." A click at the other end told me I was alone.

I put down the instrument with slow care, suddenly aware that my hands were shaking slightly. Ten o'clock. I looked at my strapwatch. Six hours yet. Either I had to find out just who this "Max" was and where he had my wife, or I must wait all those hours before I could do anything about getting her back.

A liquid groan reached my ears from across the room. I looked up in time to see Nekko, moving weakly on the floor like a dying insect. I walked over and caught him by the collar and yanked him to his feet. "Last chance, sweetheart," I said. "Where do I find Max?"

He hung there, his eyes glazed, his mouth slack, and said nothing. I brought up the .32 and raked the sight across one cheek, laying it open to the bone. "Give, damn you! Where do I find Max?"

Pain took the vacant look from his eyes and brought a groan from his tortured lungs. The battered lips writhed, forming words that were too faint and indistinct for me to interpret. I put my ear close to his mouth. "Tell me again."

". . . warehouse . . . full . . . radio . . ."

Bright blood came spilling from his mouth and he went slack in my grasp. I stared at the blood, realizing it was arterial blood. Something had given way inside of him from the treatment he had taken; perhaps a broken rib had punctured a lung as the result of his being hit by the thrown chair.

He died in my hands. I let the body slip to the floor and went back to the desk. Nekko's last words had been too vague to be useful. "A warehouse full of radios" could have meant anything. I tackled the desk again, looking for a lead.

At the end of half an hour I had gone through those three offices as thoroughly as it is possible to go through anything. No file of private phone numbers, no personal papers of any kind. Only a lot of bills of lading, invoices, etc., on miscellaneous merchandise being shipped abroad.

I was at the washbasin in the center office when the phone rang again. Before it could ring a second time I was in there and lifting the receiver. I took a slow breath and said, "Max?"

"Yeah, Luke." Nothing distinctive about the voice. "You hear from Porkov?"

"Bring her to his apartment. Ten tonight." I tried desperately to think of a question that would help me and not make him suspicious. The slightest doubt in his mind could ruin everything. But before I could come up with something, the voice said, "Check," and I was holding a dead wire.

I returned to the center office and looked at my face in the mirror over the washbasin. There was a bruise on my right cheek and a slight discoloration under one eye. I rinsed the taste of blood from my mouth, washed a few evil-smelling spots from my coat lapel and went back to wipe fingerprints off the furniture and the file cabinets. The two dead men lay where they had fallen. Sight of the man called Nekko brought his words back to me. "Warehouse full of radios." It was entirely possible that Lodi was being held in some warehouse, but the fact that there were radios in that warehouse was no help at all.

A faint memory nagged at the back of my brain. Somewhere in Nekko's last words was a key—a key that tied in with a piece of information I had picked up during the day. I went over it again, word by word. "Warehouse" . . . a blank. "Full" . . . just as blank. "Radios" . . . I frowned. Was it "radios" or "radio"? All right, so it was one radio. That made no more sense than—

And then the missing piece fell into place. Eddie Treeglos had told me earlier in the day that Ann Fullerton had died in a fire at a radio company—the *Full*bright Radio Company!

I grabbed the Manhattan telephone directory and leafed through to the right page. No listing for Fullbright Radio. The classified directory drew the same blank. But there had to be a—wait! The company was supposed to have burned out; the fire that had "killed" Ann Fullerton.

I dialed Eddie Treeglos. "Eddie, that Fullbright Radio outfit you told me about. I can't find them listed in the latest phone books. See what you can find. I'll hang on."

He came back almost immediately. "1220 Huber Street. A few blocks below Canal Street. 1220 would be damn near in the Hudson River."

I put back the receiver, used my handkerchief to wipe away the prints and went out into the corridor. Nobody around. I took the stairs to the third floor, stopped off there and rang for the elevator. The moment I heard the heavy door clang shut on the first floor, I trotted down the steps. The cage was still up there when I went out the front door to the street.

My watch showed the time as 4:45 and the sun was still high and still hot. I walked back through the heat and the stink to where I had left the convertible. It was still there and still intact. Considering the neighborhood, it could have been otherwise. I got in and drove on down to Huber Street.

VIII

It was a small narrow building of ancient red brick crammed in between a cold storage warehouse and a moving and van outfit. The front entrance was boarded up and the smoke-grimed bricks told the story. A wooden sign below the broken second-floor window read: Fullbright Radio Corp. It looked about ready to fall into the street.

I drove on by and turned the corner. Halfway along was the entrance to an alley. I parked well above it and got out. Sunlight glittered on the river's oily swell across the way. A pair of piers jutted out into the water, pointed like daggers at the Jersey shore. In one of the slips a rusty freighter stood high out of the water, its hold empty of cargo. The reek of hot tar made my nose twitch in protest.

A few doors above the alley was a hole-in-the-wall smoke shop with two shirt-sleeved men in front of it consulting a racing form. I walked past them, turning my head to look at a sun-bleached advertisement for La Palina cigars in the window. The two men didn't look up. I would have had to eat oats and run five-and-a-half furlongs in 1:03 first.

This alley was cleaner than my last one. Wire refuse containers were piled high with empty cartons and there was the clean odor of excelsior. A panel truck was backed up to the loading platform of the cold storage plant, but the driver was nowhere in sight. A few steps more and the fire-blackened rear of the Fullbright Radio Corporation was where I could reach it.

Two windows on either side of a strong-looking door. The windows still had their glass and bars besides, and the door had a new look. I went over and leaned against it and delicately tried the latch. My first break. It was unlocked.

After a long succession of bad breaks, a good one makes you suspicious. I chewed a lip, hesitating. I looked both ways along the alley. Empty as a campaign promise. I let the door swing inward a foot or two and peered through. A big room that went all the way to the front of the building, strewn with fire-blackened timbers, wrecked partitions and charred furniture. The acrid odor found after a building burns, no matter how long after, bit into my lungs. I stepped inside and closed the door, breathing lightly, and looked around. A warped metal door in one of the side walls had a floor indicator over it, but I was reasonably sure the elevator would be out of order. Even if it wasn't, the sound would alarm anybody in the place—and I didn't want to alarm anybody. Not even me.

I picked my way gingerly through the wreckage until I was nearly to the front of the building.

A narrow staircase hugged one wall, its banister sagging.

What had once been a strip of carpeting covering treads and risers was now little more than flame-chewed threads.

It looked strong enough. I went up one flight, using the balls of my feet only and staying close to the wall. At the top things looked much better than they had downstairs, although the smell was as strong. There was a line of wooden and glass partitions, with a desk, a filing case and three chairs in each where the salesmen took orders from wholesalers. Or so I figured it out. The glass on several of the partitions was broken, but that was the only damage.

I prowled the entire floor and found no sign of life. I moved quietly, opening doors without a sound and closing them the same way. Nothing.

The third floor was split by a wooden partition that extended clear to the ceiling. The half I was in had been completely cleared out, leaving bare boards and a layer of dust you could write your name in if there was nothing better to do. I stood at the top of the steps and eyed a closed door in that partition. I could see no reason for the door being closed. You have a fire and the boys with the ladders and the gleaming axes come and put out the flames and hack a few holes and go away. Then you haul out what is left and move it down the stairs and away and that's all there is to it.

Why go around closing doors?

I took out my gun and went over to the door. No sound came through it. I turned the knob slowly and pushed it open carefully. Not very far open. Just far enough to see the broad back of a man playing solitaire at a table under a shaded light globe hanging from a ceiling cord.

Against a side wall was a daybed and on the bed, her back to me, lay a woman fully dressed. I didn't need to see her face. It was Lodi. Lodi, whose beauty of face and figure was beyond the dreams of man once that initial shock had passed.

Lodi, whose secret I had managed to keep from the prying eyes of the civilized world; Lodi, who had given up so much to be with the man she loved.

I slipped into the room and came silently up behind the man at the table. He laid a black seven on a red eight with clumsy care, studied the next card in the pile, then peeled three more from those in his hand.

I said, "You could use the ace of clubs."

He jumped a foot and started to rise. I hit him on the back of the head with the gun barrel and he fell face down on the table, out cold.

"Karl!"

Lodi was struggling to sit up, her arms tied at her back. I went over and tore away the ropes and gathered her into my arms and kissed her until she was breathless.

"What have they done to you?" I demanded finally.

She shook her head, fighting back both tears and laughter. Her long dark hair needed a comb, but for my money it had never looked lovelier. "Nothing really, Karl. They were stunned, of course, when they saw my face for the first time. I think they were even a little in awe of me. They made me get dressed and brought me directly here."

"How many of them actually saw you?"

"What does it matter, darling?" She shivered. "Let's leave this horrible place. They'll be—"

"No," I said. "I've got to know."

"Four, Karl. The blonde girl and those two strange men with her and the man you found here."

"They ask you questions?"

She shrugged. "Something about a machine and they seemed to know about the rays. At least the girl did. I pretended I couldn't understand her."

My own gun was back under my arm. I took the late Mr.

Nekko's .32 out of my coat pocket and said, "Wait for me at the top of the stairs, Lodi. I've got a matter to take care of before I leave."

Her luminous eyes were troubled. "You're not going to kill him. Karl?"

"He saw you," I said flatly.

"But people will find out some day, darling. They're bound to. You can't go around—"

Her voice faltered and broke. She was staring past me, fear suddenly filling her eyes. A voice said, "Let the gun fall, my friend."

The .32 dropped from my hand and I turned slowly. It wasn't the guard after all. Standing in the doorway were the same two men who had accompanied the blonde to my home the night before. Both were holding guns.

I said, "Relax," and showed them my empty hands. The slim one gestured at the man lying half across the table and said, "Wake him up, Stephan." There was a faintly foreign sound to the words.

The burly one of the pair lowered his gun and started toward the table. The other said in the same bored tone, "Turn around, both of you," to Lodi and me, and allowed the gun in his hand to sag slightly.

I moved my hand and the .45 was out from under my arm and speaking with authority. The first slug struck Gregory above the nose and tore away half his head; the second one ripped the entire throat out of the guard, who had chosen that second to sit erect; the third caught Stephan as he was pulling the trigger of his own gun. Something made an angry sound past my ear and buried itself in the wall behind me with a dull *thunk*.

Blood, bodies and the smell of cordite. Lodi was swaying, her face buried in her hands. I picked up her light cape and the hat with the long heavy veil lying on a table next to the bed and said, "Get into these, quick. We'll have to move fast if we're going to leave before the cops get here."

She obeyed me numbly and we went quickly through the door and down the two flights of steps. Faces peered through the broken windows at the front of the building and somebody yelled at us.

We ran swiftly through the mounds of rubble to the rear door. I opened it and looked out. The alley appeared as empty of life as before. The panel truck was still backed up to the loading platform next door. I turned and beckoned to Lodi, and when I turned around again, five calm-faced men with drawn guns stepped from behind the truck to face us.

"Take it kind of easy, Mr. Terris," one of them said mildly. "We're government officers."

IX

The committee meeting was called for 10:00 A.M. at one of the hearing rooms in the Senate Building. Lodi and I got there about fifteen minutes early, escorted by a couple of extra-polite agents from the FBI.

Senator McGill was already in the waiting room outside. His mane of white hair didn't look quite as neat as usual and his heavy face was more red than florid.

He was upset enough to forget to shake hands. "Karl! My God, man, do you realize what a bad time you've given me?" He stared curiously at Lodi, who was heavily veiled, her arms covered with white gloves that ended under the sleeves of a long, high-necked dress. "Good morning, Mrs. Terris," he said, civilly enough. "I hear you've had something of a bad time of it. I do hope you're fully recovered."

105

"Thank you," Lodi said shortly.

He drew me to one side. "Don't hold anything back from them, Karl," he pleaded in an undertone. "They're sore as hell. Unless you can do some mighty tall explaining, you're going to be charged with everything from murder to spitting on the sidewalk! The way you were moving around, I'm surprised they even found you."

"I discovered how they did it," I said. "Granger, the FBI man I tied up out at the house, knew what car I was using. They put the license number on the police radio and some squad spotted it parked near Huber Street. There were a dozen Feds in the block ten minutes later, and the sound of shooting did the rest."

The door to the hearing room opened and a young man beckoned to us. I took Lodi by the arm and we walked in and sat down at a long table. Across from us were several dignified-looking men in conservative business suits. Two of them I already knew: Millard Cavendish, the ranking member of the AEC; and Winston Blake, a sharp-featured bantam rooster of a man, who wore elevator shoes and sported a black-ribboned pince-nez. Blake and I had taken an instant dislike to each other the first time we met, shortly after my return from Africa, and I knew he would be out for my scalp this time for sure.

Millard Cavendish sounded a gavel and brought the meeting to order. He was a tall, thin man with deep hollows under his cheeks and a shock of iron-grey hair that kept sliding down over his high forehead. He said, "Your name is Karl Terris and you reside in Clinton Township, Catskill County, in the State of New York. Is that correct?"

I looked at the girl behind the stenotype machine and said, "That is correct."

At this point, Winston Blake, who had been staring hard at

Lodi, cut in to say, "Mr. Cavendish, will you order this woman to remove her veil? I see no reason why she should keep her face covered during this hearing."

Before Cavendish could open his mouth, I said, "That veil stays on, Blake."

The little man bristled. "Speak when you're spoken to, sir! We're running this hearing."

"Then go ahead and run it. But the veil stays on."

Cavendish said quietly, "This is a hearing, Mr. Blake, not a style symposium. Let's get on with this, shall we?"

"I think Mr. Terris should be reminded," Blake snapped, "that it is within the province of this committee to cite a witness for contempt."

"Let's hope," I said, "that none of its members gives me a reason for being contemptuous."

Behind me somebody smothered a chuckle. Blake's face turned a fiery red. The gavel smacked its block once and Cavendish said, "Mr. Terris, you appeared before this committee some six weeks ago upon your unexpected return from Africa after an absence of two years. At the time of your disappearance you were, as a volunteer, engaged in mapping an area of French Equatorial Africa by air for the United States Government. The purpose of this aerial survey was to locate unusually rich deposits of fissionable material believed to be somewhere in that locality. Am I correct thus far?"

"Yes, sir."

"In your appearance before this committee earlier you stated, under oath, that you failed to locate such deposits, that you had no idea where, if at all, they were located, and that the photographs taken of the locality had been destroyed at the time your plane crashed. This, too, is correct?"

"Yes, sir."

Cavendish fixed me with a not unkindly eye. "Do you, at

this time, wish to enlarge on that testimony?"

"No, sir."

The chairman picked up a sheet of paper from a thin sheaf next to his right elbow, studied it briefly, then put it down and looked sharply at me. "Mr. Terris," he said, "twelve days ago a Mr. and Mrs. Clarence Mather died under mysterious circumstances in the south of France. An examination showed both had died of being exposed to cosmic radiation of a highly concentrated form. Exposure took place, it has been established, between thirty and thirty-five days before their deaths. Further investigation revealed that the couple was aboard the tramp steamer *City of Stockholm* at the time of such exposure. Now, it is a matter of record that you chartered the *City of Stockholm* at the port of Dakar, in Africa, for the purpose of transporting you and your wife to America. Furthermore, the cabin you and your wife occupied during the crossing was the one occupied immediately afterward by Mr. and Mrs. Mather. An immediate investigation was made of the ship and your cabin by qualified scientists, and a faint but unmistakable trace of radiation was found therein. By this time the radiation was far too slight to harm anyone, but the fact remains that it was found therein. In view of these facts, and in view of the purpose behind your original visit to Africa, this committee again asks if you wish to correct your previous testimony."

"No, sir."

There was a general shuffling of feet and shifting of chairs by the rest of the committee. Blake leaned toward the man to his left and whispered something in his ear. The two of them engaged Cavendish in a muttered colloquy pitched too low for me to hear, even if I had wanted to, which I didn't.

Senator McGill bent over me.

"Damn it, Karl, what are you trying to pull? They've got

108

enough evidence to pin perjury on you ten times over! This is your country; why aren't you willing to help it?"

I looked up at him. "Senator, if anyone's going to teach me patriotism, it won't be you. Now kindly get the hell away from me!"

Lodi reached over and put a gloved hand on my arm and squeezed it understandingly. Behind the heavy veil she was watching me, I knew, with deep concern.

Millard Cavendish had concluded his discussion with the rest of the committee members. He looked me directly in the eye and the lines of his face were stern.

"I have some questions to ask you, Mr. Terris. Please let me remind you that this committee is empowered to ask these questions and to demand a truthful answer to each. Is that clear?"

"Perfectly."

He nodded shortly. "I will ask you, Mr. Terris, if you brought into this country, at any time a device or machine having to do with cosmic radiation or energy?"

"No, sir."

A wrinkle deepened between his eyes. "Then how do you explain what happened to the Mathers and the finding of the experts who examined your cabin on the *City of Stockholm*?"

"That, Mr. Cavendish," I said, "would be a matter of conjecture on my part. I recognize this committee's right to ask me questions, but I do not believe it can demand conjectures."

The wrinkle became a frown. "Then I will ask you, sir: do you know how the cosmic radiation got into that cabin?"

"The question," I said, "is do I *know* how the radiation got into that cabin. The answer is no."

Winston Blake said, "This man is deliberately evasive. I say he should be cited for contempt for his last remark, and for every succeeding remark of its kind."

"Is that supposed to intimidate me?" I asked.

The gavel came down, hard. Cavendish said, "Let's keep our tempers, gentlemen. . . . Mr. Terris, while you were in Africa, did you come into contact with any device, manufactured or natural that had to do with cosmic radiations or energy?"

"I did."

It took a moment for the reply to get a reaction. There was a sudden babble of voices behind me and the members of the committee stiffened in their chairs. Cavendish rapped several times before order was restored.

He said sternly, "As a patriotic American, Mr. Terris, you must have a sound reason for withholding such information from your country. This committee would like to hear that reason."

I said, "I yield to no one on the strength of my patriotism. But I'm not going to confuse patriotism with chauvinism. By revealing the location of the machines used in controlling and concentrating cosmic energy, I would bring death and destruction not only to a peaceful and innocent people but to the rest of the world."

Millard Cavendish sighed. "This nation is not a warlike one, Mr. Terris. Possession of this secret, judging from what you say, would make America so powerful that no other nation, or coalition of nations, would dare launch a war."

I laughed shortly. "Secret weapons as a deterrent to war are useful only as long as they are controlled by one nation. Need I remind you that spies invariably manage to get their hands on such weapons and peddle them to other nations?"

Winston Blake said, "I'm getting tired of this nonsense." He leaned across the table and stabbed me with his chill blue eyes. "I'll put this in words of one syllable for you, Terris. We want this secret and we want it now. Either you give us the exact location of these devices, or whatever they are, or you'll be branded a traitor to your country in the eyes and ears of every one of your fellow Americans. You're a rich man, I'm told. Well, this is one time your wealth isn't going to save you."

I said, "It's fatheads like you that guarantee my silence."

His face turned a violent crimson and for a moment I thought he was on the verge of a stroke. "I want this man arrested!" he bellowed. "I'll show him he can't vilify a member of this body and get away—"

The banging of the gavel cut him off. Cavendish said frostily, "Mr. Blake is ready for your apology, Mr. Terris."

"Then let him earn it," I said, just as frostily. "I don't have to take that kind of talk from him or anybody else."

By this time Blake was on his feet. "I see no reason to continue questioning this witness. His reasons for refusing to turn over to us such vital information are patently the usual Communist Party line. A man like this deserves to be named a traitor—and if we can't make that stick, let him answer for his unprovoked assault on an agent of the Federal Bureau of Investigation, as well as the brutal slaying of six men in something less than twenty-four hours."

Beside me, Lodi spoke for the first time. "Tell them what they want to know, Karl. It doesn't matter."

I stared at her, aghast. "You don't know what you're saying! Do you want your people to go through what the rest of the world has suffered? Have you forgotten what happened to them that first time?"

Her voice was firm. "You know the kind of protection my people have, Karl. Ten thousand planes couldn't find our city in hundreds of years if they didn't want to be found. Tell these men the whole story. I don't want the man I love to be hated by his own country."

I placed a hand lightly on her veil. "Do you want them to know about you? Do you want this veil stripped away for the world to see? Do you want to be laughed at, shunned, hear every so-called comedian toss off a collection of gag lines about you?"

"It doesn't matter, Karl. Your real reason for refusing them is your wish to protect me, not my people. I know that, and it must not be that way. All that does matter is your love for me."

They were listening to us. The room was silent as a morgue. I took a deep slow breath. "Is that the way you want it, Lodi?"

"Yes."

I rose from the chair and look at the men behind the table. "Okay," I said. "I'm going to tell you a story. It's a story I want the world to hear from my lips, not to learn through a lot of distorted secondhand accounts. Bring in the newsmen and the spectators."

"We're running this, Terris," Winston Blake said coldly. "I see no reason to—"

"You're not running it now," I said. "Either I tell it my way or you can sweat turpentine and not get a word out of me. It's strictly up to you."

An almost invisible smile was tugging at Millard Cavendish's fine lips. He said, "I suggest a compromise. Newsmen, yes; but no spectators. Any part of Mr. Terris' story that can be a threat to our national security will not be published. Is that satisfactory to you, Mr. Terris?"

Once more I looked at Lodi. She nodded ever so slightly. I said. "Bring 'em in and let's get this over with."

It required only a few minutes before the press seats were filled. Curious eyes bored into us, but more of them were on the veiled woman next to me than anywhere else. Cavendish rapped his gavel lightly once and said, "We're ready to hear you, sir."

I stood there, bending forward slightly, one hand resting on the table. I said:

"Two years ago, I crashed my plane in an African jungle hundreds of miles from civilization. The reason for my being in that part of the world is known to everybody. I was injured in the crash and lay at the edge of a clearing for hours in great pain before I finally blacked out. When I came to, I found myself in a vast underground city, attended by the kindest, most generous people who ever lived. These people nursed me back to health and made me one of them. They trusted me, and when I fell in love with the daughter of their ruling family, they gave her to me as my wife.

"I learned the history of this race. Many thousands of years ago this race lived in four great cities on the surface of the Earth. These were cities of great beauty, of towering spires and luxurious homes. The rest of the Earth was just emerging from the Paleolithic Age, and nothing broke the peace and contentment of their lives.

"And then one day a vast armada of airships swooped down on these peaceful people. Bombs leveled the four cities and those who did not die were taken away as captives. When the enemy finally left, the few survivors sought refuge in underground caves."

Everybody in the room was hanging on my words. A few of the reporters were taking notes, but most of them simply listened with open mouths. I took a couple of steps down the room and came back and stood there, resting a hand lightly on Lodi's shoulder.

"These people I'm telling you about," I went on, "had the knowledge of great power. They knew how to harness cosmic

113

rays—a force sufficient to blow this globe of ours into atoms. They could have constructed weapons that would make the H-bomb something, by comparison, you could shoot off in your fingers!

"But they used this power for more important things. With it they illuminated their caves to the brilliance of sunlight. As the centuries passed, their numbers increased until the population was back to where it had been at the time the attack had come. But they chose to remain underground, so that never again would they be attacked; and except for a few surface guards, none of them ventured out of those caves."

I paused again, this time to look at the three men across the table from me. Cavendish was leaning back in his chair, staring fixedly at my face; Blake was staring down at the pince-nez in his hand; Rasmussen, the third man, sat with his chin resting on one palm. The silence was absolute.

"One of those surface guards found me," I said. "Instead of killing me, he brought me to safety. I grew to love those people, made one of them my wife, and through her and them I knew happiness for the first time in my life.

"But there was one factor I forgot to take into consideration, gentlemen. We call it homesickness. I wanted to go back, to leave that paradise, for the doubtful benefits of what we call civilization. And against my better judgment, knowing exactly what it would mean to her, I brought Lodi with me."

I stopped long enough to pour water into a glass and drink it, then lit a cigarette and went on:

"This brings me to something I failed to mention earlier. These people had learned the secret of longevity. I knew men and women three and four hundred years old who looked and acted younger than I did!"

A murmur of astonishment and open doubt ran through

the room. I kept right on talking, getting it all out before my vocal cords gave up:

"Cosmic radiations were the answer. Ages of exposure to those rays had resulted in an inherent immunity to harmful effects. Once every fourteen days each of these people exposed himself to a full charge of the energy; by doing so old age was held back. But after such exposure they gave off for a few days rays that would kill any ordinary man who came in contact with them. They knew this, of course; I was given a series of injections immediately to keep the emanations from harming me.

"There's not much left to tell you, gentlemen. Lodi went with me in my repaired plane. We landed near Dakar the following day; I chartered a ship for our trip to America. Unknown to me, however, Lodi had exposed herself to the customary charge of cosmic energy shortly before we left her people. As long as she wore proper clothing no one would be harmed; but by undressing in her cabin, she left a concentration of the rays. By the time we reached this country she was no longer a threat to other people; but the Mathers were unfortunate enough to occupy the cabin too soon afterward."

I spread my hands. "Except for one more incident, that's the story. The incident concerns a group of Communist agents who learned what had caused the Mathers' deaths. They assumed I had brought back a machine that produced cosmic energy, and to force me to turn it over to them they kidnapped my wife. In getting her back, I'm afraid, a few people got hurt. It makes for a nice touch: in kidnapping my wife to force me into giving them the machine, they had the machine all along!"

I sat down and knocked the ash from my cigarette gently into a tray. No one said anything for almost a minute. Then

Winston Blake carefully lifted his pince-nez and placed it firmly astride his nose.

"Of all the arrant nonsense I ever heard," he snarled, "this concoction I've just listened to takes the prize. By what evolutionary freak did a race of people shoot up ahead of cavemen to produce the wonders you told us about? And this air raid; I suppose it came from Saturn!"

I shook my head politely. "No, sir. From Venus. And evolution had nothing to do with the people of the caves, Mr. Blake. They came originally from Mars!"

I got out of my chair and helped Lodi to her feet. "You want proof, Mr. Blake. Then by God you'll get proof!"

Before any of them realized what was happening, I tore away the veil covering Lodi's face, then hooked my fingers under the high neckline of her dress and ripped it and the underclothing beneath completely from her lush and lovely body.

"Go ahead, you lousy ghouls," I said. "Take a good look!"

The collective gasp was like the rustling of a strong breeze. For the skin of the most beautiful woman of two worlds was a rich and luminous green!

X

It was after two o'clock by the time we drove into New York City and by that time the newspapers were out with the story. At Lodi's insistence I stopped at a stand and bought two of them. The banner head on the *Gazette* said: "HOW GREEN WAS MY MARTIAN," and the managing editor had made his bid for a salary increase by having the words printed in green ink. The *Standard* headline was less imaginative but more factual: "TERRIS MYSTERY BRIDE FROM MARS!"

We were nearly to the Westchester county line before Lodi put aside the papers and leaned back to let the air cool her burning cheeks. I said. "That's only a small sample, baby. They'll crucify you from now on."

"I don't mind, Karl. If you don't."

"You'll mind," I said. "You'd have to have the skin of a rhinoceros not to mind. To the rest of the world you're a freak and freaks pay a high price for living."

"Will it matter so much to you, Karl?"

"It won't get a chance to," I said harshly. "We're going back, Lodi. Back to your people for the rest of our lives. I've had enough of my kind; let them blow themselves to hell and I'll like it fine."

She laid one of her delicate hands over mine on the wheel. "They are your people, darling. You can't run out on them, on the responsibilities your great wealth gives you. You'd be terribly unhappy before long."

It was my turn to squeeze *her* hand. "Not as long as we're together, Lodi."

After several miles of silence, Lodi said, "At least they're not going to try to find where my people are."

"Not after they got the details of the power they'd be up against," I said. "The theory of the rest of the world will be: 'Let sleeping dogs lie'—no matter how tempted any nation gets to pull a fast one."

Shortly before five-thirty I swung off the Taconic Parkway and followed the private road on up the hill to the house. The late afternoon sun dappled the lawn through the trees and a tired breeze moved the leaves with a whispering sound. Lodi opened the car door and picked up her veil preparatory to getting out.

I said, "Forget the veil, baby. You'll never wear it again."

She smiled, the slow warm smile that had knocked me for

a loop the first time I'd seen it. "You're sure you want it to be that way, Karl?"

"Absolutely."

She left it lying crumpled on the seat and we went up the porch steps together. I unlocked the front door and followed her into the entrance hall—and a tall slender blond man stepped from behind the short wall of the dining room and pointed a gun at us.

He flashed his teeth and said, "I was beginning to think you hadn't paid the rent. Close the door, please—and keep your hands away from your body."

He looked like a Swedish diplomat, all right, and there were the three pock marks high up on his left cheek. Sergi Porkov. It couldn't have been anyone else. And just to wrap it up for sure, Ann Fullerton, in figured crepe silk that did a lot for her wheat-field hair, appeared in the opening behind him. She was carrying a good-sized patent-leather bag under one arm and she looked cool and neat and very, very lovely.

I started to say something but Porkov cut me off with a small gesture of the gun. From where I stood I judged it to be one of the old model Walther P-38's. Not exactly a cannon, but at the moment he didn't need a cannon. He said, "I think you had better lift your hands quite high and turn around. Both of you. Slowly."

We had a choice. We could turn around or we could refuse—and get shot down on the spot. We turned. He slithered up behind me and let a soft meaty hand prowl my body. He was smart enough to hold the gun so that it actually wasn't against me. He snaked out the .45 from under my arm, made sure it was the only weapon I carried, then went to work on Lodi. She couldn't have hidden a penknife in what she was wearing, but that didn't keep him from trying. I heard her gasp slightly a time or two, and while my muscles crawled I kept them from getting away from me.

He finally stepped back. "I think we will go up the stairs now. In case of unexpected visitors."

We went up the stairs and into the sitting room between the two master bedrooms. Porkov waved us into a couple of the lounge chairs there and then sat down on the edge of one across from Lodi and me. The Fullerton girl remained near the hall door, just standing there looking a little pale, a pinched expression around her full lips.

Lodi leaned back in her chair and folded her hands. She had the Oriental trick of turning completely impassive when things weren't going right. Porkov crossed his legs and wagged the gun carelessly at her. "Green or not," he said admiringly, "you're still the best-looking woman I've ever seen."

I said, "Maybe you'd like to change off for a night or two."

He turned his teeth on again. "It is a thought. Rather a good one. But I'm afraid not. No. I have other plans for your very charming and very beautiful green wife."

I said, "I'd like a cigarette."

"By all means! Perhaps your wife would like a last one also."

From the doorway Ann Fullerton said, "Sergi! You're not—"

Without turning his head he said, "Shut up! Speak when you're spoken to."

I lit a cigarette for Lodi and one for myself. My hands weren't shaking, but not because they didn't want to. I said, "So you're going to pull the string on us. I wonder why. Not for the secret machine, I'm sure. You must have read all about that in the papers by this time."

He swung his crossed leg idly. "No, my friend. Not the machine. We slipped badly on that, Ann and I. No; you took the lives of six of the men associated with me. In effect, you made a fool out of me as well. This last is unforgivable, Mr. Terris."

"Then you won't accept my apology?"

He eyed me almost admiringly. "You are a brave man, sir. I like brave men. . . . Tell me. Mr. Terris, do you love your wife?"

". . . We weren't planning on getting a divorce."

He nodded, satisfied. "I don't intend to kill you, my friend. Not, that is, unless you literally force me to—which you may well do. It will be an interesting experiment, this—to learn if grief can drive a man to ignoring the law of self-preservation. I know it has done that to some men."

"I haven't the slightest idea," I said, "what the hell you're talking about."

He bent forward across his knee. "Killing you, sir, would accomplish nothing. As they say, your troubles would be over. Dead men feel nothing: no pain, no anguish of soul, no regrets. But when a man loses the one thing he holds most dear, something he has suffered for, endured hardship for, fought for—that loss is, to him, more horrible even than death. In your particular case, Terris, it would be your wife."

Something with cold feet walked up my spine. I bit down on my teeth, and it was almost a minute before my throat could form words. "You can't afford another mistake, Porkov. You'll take a full helping of hell if you so much as start a run in one of my wife's stockings. People who know me will tell you that."

He said, "You fascinate me, Mr. Terris," and lifted the gun and shot Lodi three times through the left breast.

Through a twisting nightmare of incredulity I watched my wife droop like a tired flower. Then her body sagged forward and she toppled out of the chair to form a pathetic heap on the rug. Death had been instantaneous.

I stood up the way an old, old man stands up. I started toward Porkov. I was in no hurry. I wouldn't live to reach his throat anyway. But that was where I was going.

From the doorway, Ann Fullerton took a gun out of her bag and shot Porkov through the head. Before he hit the floor she was standing over him, pulling the trigger again and again. He caught the full load and even after the gun was empty she went on pulling the trigger in a frenzy of hatred and revulsion until I took it gently out of her fingers.

She turned on me, her eyes burning, her breasts shaking, her body trembling. "I killed him, Karl. I love you! I want you! Right here! Now! Now!"

You don't explain those things. Not at the time, nor later. Nor ever. The blood sang through me and her body was hotter than any fire and mine was just as hot.

I was sitting on the bed when she came out of the shower. She was as naked as the palm of a baby's hand and she smelled of bath powder. She came over and sat down on the bed beside me and put both arms around me.

"We'll put all those other things out of our minds, Karl, darling." Her voice was like the purr of a cat. "I loved you from the first moment I saw you. We'll go away, Karl, and we'll have each other, and that will be all we'll ever want. Just us two. . . ."

I didn't say anything. She got up and went over to the vanity and began to run the comb through her hair. She was what the boys who invented Valhalla were talking about. She had a body that would melt a glacier from across the street. She was everything a man wanted in a woman if all he wanted was a body.

Very slowly I reached under the pillow and took out the

.45. I held it loosely in one hand and raised my head and said, "Turn around, Ann."

She turned around and saw the gun and all the color ran out of her face. "No, darling. No! I killed him, Karl. I killed the man who shot your wife. He would have killed you too. I saved your life!"

I said. "Sure, baby, you did fine," and fired twice. She caught both slugs full in the belly. I could hear them go in from clear across the room.

I put the gun down and smiled a little looking at her. I said, "The worms will love you, darling," and got up and walked over to the telephone.

I wondered what the cops would say about finding her naked that way.

The Affair with the Dragon Lady

Now that that wise guy photographer from *Life* found us out there's hardly any sense making up excuses for what happened. We might sound like a pack of idiots to some, but, damn it all, for two whole years we had a lot of fun with our secret society and crazy clubhouse and in a way it's a shame to see it all end.

Only watch out who you call crazy, because you'd be surprised at the big names who put on the *Dragon Lady* costume for one of the meetings and tucked same costume away in a locked trunk in the attic and hoped for another invite back.

Like all good things, though, it had to come to an end. And, like most good things, it took a dame and a calamity to bring it about, so now our secret society is out in the open where all can see it and to save wear and tear on the tarmac I'll tell you about it.

The story really starts back in October of '45 and you know how that was. All of us coming out of the service all at once with a pocket full of dough, if you were lucky, and plenty of places to spend it. If you were lucky enough to be married, you settled down right away. If you weren't, you made all the places, saw all the faces, joined the 52-20 club until you got a job, and from then on wondered what had happened to three or four years and didn't know whether to be sad or glad about being in civvies.

123

Well, there we were, the ten husbands of the *Dragon Lady*. Our mutual wife was a B-17E with bullet-hole acne, a patched-up tail, and joints that creaked and groaned even when she was trying to rest. Still, she was a thing of beauty who took us all there and back 82 times, twice almost giving her own life in a grand gesture that we might live, but survived because our love for her was just as strong.

You can imagine having to leave her. We each took a little piece of her away in our B-4 bags, kissed her mutilated body, and left her there with tears of 100 octane dripping from No. 1 and No. 4 engines. Don't ever tell us an airplane can't cry.

We did, too, because, behind us, strangers took her to a far away prison in the desert with others of her kind, put her in solitary confinement behind plastic shrouds and left her there to die in whatever strange way airplanes are supposed to die.

Us? We all came home to the same state, settled down within three counties of each other and began the slow disintegrating process of living. We all wrote, sent greeting cards, got drunk, and went phone happy sometimes, but we stayed in touch. From Ed Parcey, the tail gunner, up to me as first pilot, we all had babies a few times, named them after each other until you could hardly tell who from whom on the roster.

That is, all of us except Vern Tice, our old co-pilot who out and out refused to enter the marital state because he didn't want to get like us. Which is to say, weathered out of our own desires by women who made better mothers than wives and wanted the same thing from both children and husbands alike.

Hell, it's an old story, why repeat it?

Charlie Cross, our engineer, and I wanted to operate a rice-seeding outfit using Stearmans. The wives cried us out of it. Henry Lucerne, the navigator, Vic Cabot, the radioman, and "Tiny" Sinkwich, who handled the right waist gun, were going to patent and manufacture an electronic homing device for private planes.

That meant a few initial hardships, the giving up of minor, but stable, positions and the women sulked them out of that. Needless to say, somebody else invented and sold the same thing and made a fortune, but when you mentioned it to the girls you only got a frosty stare.

Lou Kubitsky, the other waist gunner, didn't do too badly. Before the war he was a fighter and, had he gone back into it, he would have had his head knocked off. Instead, he became a grocer and, when the community developed, his store was in the center of it and he made out just great. He was happy, all right, but he sure hated groceries. So on the side he managed a couple of fighters, sparred with them and kept his hand in.

George Poe, Arnie Castle, and Fred Halloway were salesmen for the same firm of Coster and Selig, Printers, lived in the same northeast sector of the suburbs, borrowed each other's tools, and looked to the sky whenever a prop job went over, and studiously ignored the blowjobs as interlopers. Each had a wife who had sweated out all 82 missions and to whom even talk of flying was anathema.

So there we were, all paramours of the *Dragon Lady*, and, with one exception, no longer bold, but getting old. And when that lone exception showed up it meant a lot of fun for a while as long as you could take a week of cold silences, too-casual meals, and a few other things pouting women can conjure up.

Which brings us back to Vern Tice again.

He was 38 last year, still in good shape with hardly any grey showing and no sign of fat, good-looking as always, with a mint in his back pocket he had picked up on speculative deals most smart money stayed away from. His big deal was banking a Broadway show for 50 percent that gave him a gigantic return with a year and a half run. But women? Oh, he loved 'em all. Marry one? After seeing the trap we were all in?

Laugh, laugh.

That's the way things stood the day old Vern blew in driving a white Jag with the leading lady of *Fielder's Choice* next to him. She was a big blonde beaut dripping diamonds and furs with a laugh like ice clinking in a highball and without her as a come-on we never would have made the briefing because it was an axiom among the women that we should never all get together at the same time.

Elaine Hood fixed that. Every one of the girls wanted a look at this fabulous creature who was all over the covers of current magazines and in most of the gossip columns every week. Smart boy, that Vern. He had checked her out well on her procedures, then let her solo in this strange world of suburbanism.

One thing about her. She was ready for combat right off. She didn't go into it with her head up and locked, not a bit. That girl had all her guns armed and went into tactical maneuvers like a 50-mission vet. The other women never had a chance, really.

So after supper at the country club they were all glad to let the boys go hang around the bar for once while they started pumping Elaine for all the latest tidbits.

Being Monday, we had the bar all to ourselves, toasted the old days a few times, then Charlie Cross said with peculiar feeling, "To the old girl herself. To the *Dragon Lady*, laddies."

We lifted our glasses to that one, all right.

When we put them down Vern said, "Miss her, don't you?"

"Come off it," George Poe said, "who doesn't? Man, I've put in a thousand missions in dreams since I saw her last."

"How'd you all like to see her again?" Vern said.

For a good ten seconds it was real quiet. If anybody else had said that there would have been the usual good-natured groans of acknowledgment, but this time it was Vern who said it and suddenly we knew what the pitch was. We *knew,* but we couldn't be quite sure.

Tiny Sinkwich turned around real slowly and put up some ack-ack. "She's long gone in some smelter's pot, buddy. That or blown up doing drone duty for rocket jockeys in F-100s."

Vern's grin went all the way across his face. "You think?"

I said, "Okay, kid, drop your flaps and take us in. You've had something cooking ever since you taxied up. Now start debriefing."

He was enjoying every second of it. He had us hanging by our shroud lines and wasn't cutting us loose until he had to. Finally he said, "I bought the *Dragon Lady.*"

"*You what?*" Charlie's voice was almost a squeak.

"That's right. I bought her. I went through surplus sales and dragged the old girl out of the pile and right now she's sitting over at the Lakemore Airfield in the big hangar as pretty as you please."

"You're crazy," I said, "Lakemore's abandoned. It's all swamp from where the water backed up from the government dam project. You couldn't put a Piper Cub in there."

Vern grinned again and nodded sagely. "I know. She went in by truck."

From down at the end where Ed Parcy guarded the tail out of sheer force of habit, he said skeptically, "There's no road into there, buddy."

Between sips of his drink Vern said, "There is now. I bought a road, too. Those steel mats they used to lay up for

127

temporary runways over sand or muck. Worked real well."

"Lakemore Airfield was owned by . . ." Vic Cabot started to say.

Then Vern cut him off with, "The Blakenship family. I bought it from them. The deed is free and clear and all ours."

I think we said it all at once. *"Ours?"*

He laughed at the expressions on our faces. "Sure. You don't think I'd keep the old dame all to myself, do you?"

Henry Lucerne said, "But . . ."

"Look," Vern told all of us. "I've watched you guys losing your lift ever since we left the *Lady.* You're all like kids with your toy taken away and those dames in there . . ." He waved a thumb over his shoulder, "won't give it back. Well, now they got trouble because we got our dame back and she's all ours."

You don't say much at a moment like that. You try to think of something but it won't come out so you have a drink to cover your astonishment and when it's down it all begins to make sense. Everybody tried to talk at once, slap each other's back and finally came to the same thought.

They left it up to me to put it into words. I said, "There's only one problem, friend. We can't fly her around. It would cost an arm and a leg for fuel and parts—and who knows if we can even get her license back?"

"So who needs to fly?" Vern asked me.

I just looked at him. In fact, we all did.

He laughed and said, "Buddies, we got ourselves the craziest clubhouse anybody ever saw on the best patch of ground for fishing and duck shooting in the whole state."

And when we thought about it, he was right.

Thus began the second saga of the *Dragon Lady.*

Elaine Hood was a real pro at her job. She hinted that if the gals "could only" take off a week she'd like to show them around the big town north of us and you never saw nine wives go to work so fast. Oh, we let them sweat a little bit and work their female wiles to the limit, but finally we okayed their flight plans, let them arrange for in-law baby sitters, and saw them all off at the station.

That same day we all started our vacations and went back to our true love, our one wife, the *Dragon Lady*, and there behind the faded and weather-worn walls of the old hangar primped and petted her until she was a thing of beauty again.

A flip of a switch would bring her to life for us. She would quiver when you touched the controls, talk to you when you pressed the mike button, and through some almost forgotten G.I. genius we could warm her belly in winter and cool it in summer.

Since we were lovers and not fighters anymore, it was appropriate to redesign the *Lady*, but she didn't mind. In fact, she seemed to welcome the change. She liked the addition of the bar and the compact gas range and oversize refrigerator. The tables and chairs fitted in just right and the TV set seemed to have always belonged there.

Oh, we kept her in character. No gaudy paint jobs when we had cans of o.d. around. Outside on her skin we tickled her with brushes and brightened up the original markings. A few of the old wounds needed to be sutured up once more and she was all the better for it.

In one week we had her laughing again and a dozen weekends later she was ours, all ours, to love and cherish as we wished. Ah, what a second honeymoon we had! It took a lot of tailoring to get into our wedding clothes again, but we got the uniforms back on, the mold off the leather, and the film off the brass.

I'm glad *Life* didn't see us then, coming out of the old tool shed that we made into a dressing room, turned out in old AAF pinks and greens and dress khakis. We saluted each other silly, patted the surplus chutes that hung from hooks under our names and slipped into the hangar under blackout conditions like back in England when we knew Jerry was upstairs looking for a target.

When the door was closed, Tiny said, "Everybody in?"

A murmur went around our heads, sounding strangely hollow in the vault of the hangar.

"Okay," Tiny said, "Flip 'er."

Vern pulled the switch, flooded the place with lights placed just so and for all the world we were back there on the stand waiting for take-off.

"Beautiful," somebody said, "just beautiful."

And in the same order, just like back in '44, we climbed aboard the *Dragon Lady* to celebrate our wedding night all over again, bringing to her gifts to show our love . . . the same little bits and pieces we had all taken away as mementos years before, gently put them back where they belonged . . . and the night was consummated in grand style.

Now that was the beginning. You can only keep a beauty like the *Lady* quiet for so long. A man just has to brag, and having done so, has to back up his talk and before long the *Dragon Lady* had an entourage the way any royal dame should. Of course, only ex-AAF personnel were invited to a "flight" on that Baker One Seven, and even then they had to conform to spec. Orders of the day said you went on board in the appropriate uniform and those who didn't have one, either borrowed Class As or dug up something in surplus.

You can bet one thing. Nobody was ever disappointed. Before long that old hangar became a lavish combination Officers' and N.C.Os' Club where men could be men in the old style, fight the war as they pleased, and forget the crazy old

130

world outside. It was the place of the Permanent Pass, the Big Open Post, the Fabulous Furlough.

Nobody was old there. When they felt that way they could find their places inside the *Dragon Lady* and she would console them within herself and give them back their youth.

Of course, Vern Tice knew what he was doing all the time. The place was paying off in grand style and, although the fees were small, all the money stayed in the barracks and finally we had a bomber base to beat all bomber bases. Never was one staffed so adequately with so much rank and so many sergeants.

Never was the location of one base so carefully guarded.

Oh, those women on the home front knew something was going on, that's for sure. They'd beg and wheedle to find out what it was, but what man in his right mind is going to give his wife the address of his mistress?

Now right here I have to mention that there was *one* woman who knew the score. That was Elaine Hood, who by now had become big in Hollywood—picked up an Oscar, but didn't pick up Vern Tice no matter how hard she tried, and believe me she tried.

Vern didn't know it, but all of us married pigeons knew it. Those already trapped can look back and see the pitfalls.

One thing you have to say about old Elaine. She never squealed. She knew all about our mistress and could have let out the big secret to the town at any time. Good kid, that one, no chicken anymore, but still lovely and with a complete sense of understanding. She became good friends with all the wives of the *Lady*'s original crew and sort of welded them together to the point where they began liking each other's company and would even stand for hangar talk over the supper table at the country club.

In fact (and we say it was because they were afraid to com-

131

pete with the *Dragon Lady*), they even helped when Tiny, Vic, and Henry pooled all their savings and started making electronic equipment. Lou Kubitsky sold his store, opened a sports arena, and made a bundle. Irene, his wife, sold tickets and loved it. Come to think of it, things like that were happening to everybody.

And back at the Happy Hangar way out there in the swamps, the fishing grew better, the duck shooting greater, and all the state would have wanted in on it had they known it was there. But it was our secret and none would give it away. Vern made his like he always did, but he wasn't so happy about it anymore. You could tell. When the flight was over and the crew left for their bunks, Vern would take off in his Jag and go prowling around. Sometimes he'd go see Elaine, but when he came back you could see he was having a struggle with himself and it took a hard month to tell some of the women to lay off the matchmaking attempts and let him and Elaine be. If the guy didn't want to get married, so let him live in a BOQ.

It was about then, at the end of summer, that two things happened simultaneously. Elaine finished her run on Broadway and the Air Force decided to reactivate Ellison Field, about 10 miles out of town. So Elaine moved into an apartment on Avery Road around the corner from us and the 332nd moved 50 F-100's into Ellison.

Those great big air-borne hogs overhead made all the kids happy and brought smiles to the faces of merchants, but to us old prop men they were just noise makers that needed too damn much runway to get off and ten times that to get back down.

But they raised hell with our hangar hours because whenever one of those blowjobs would go by overhead it made our *Dragon Lady* seem suddenly old and that was one thing we just couldn't tolerate. It got so that when we saw one of those pink-cheeked pilots on the street we'd freeze him down, him in his blues that made him look like he never got out of the kaydets.

Maybe if it hadn't been for the Vern Tice–Elaine Hood sideline show we all would have had pilot fatigue, but those two were flying the craziest kind of sidewalk formations you ever saw. Everybody but Vern knew it was love, but, even if he did know, she was the enemy to be avoided. He enjoyed the combat angle, the boy-girl stuff, but when it came to the Big Tangle, he put his nose down and hit for the barn.

My wife was the one who put her finger on it. Vern had the old gang back together again and he was afraid that marriage to Elaine would be like bailing out on the return leg of a milk run. She'd have him off in Hollywood or back on Broadway and not even a goodbye kiss for his true lady fair in the hangar, and *that* he couldn't stand.

It was right in the middle of the fall that everything came to a head. Vern and Elaine finally had it out and, from what I heard by way of eavesdropping on a phone conversation, she was going back to Hollywood to do a picture and Vern was going to stay put. I passed the word around because by now we were all on her side and hated to see Vern a permanent party in the BOQ when he could just as easily get married.

He claimed it was just a case of misery wanting company but I knew that he was talking through his hat even if he didn't admit it. And that was the way things stood the night of our anniversary party. The whole squadron had assembled to cheer up Vern, damn the interlopers at Ellison Field, and drink to our ever-loving mistress, the *Dragon Lady* who was the fairest of them all, bar none, no none at all.

Ah, yes, this was to be a night! Waldo Casey and the Stephano brothers had brought along six converts between them and, like all first timers, they had bad gaposis in their old uniforms. You never did see guys have so much fun, though.

Yeah, we were really rolling along about 8, hangar flying as usual, winning the war personally, turning all the little things into big things.

Upstairs a jet cracked the sound barrier with one hell of a bash and for a few seconds everyone stopped talking.

Maybe it was a half-hour later that the phone rang and after Tiny answered it he edged up to Vern who was talking to me and said, "It's for you, Vern."

Now nobody but nobody outside our own group has that number and this night everybody was here. That left Elaine. I watched Vern get grim around his mouth and he shook his head just once. "Tell her nix, Tiny."

Then Tiny shook his head. "Not me, buddy. She said you speak to her because this one's important. She made it stick, too."

Vern frowned a little bit. "How?"

"Brother," Tiny said, "can she use G.I. language. You better talk to her."

Vern frowned at that, shrugged, and picked up the phone, took a breath and said. "All right, chick, what's up?"

It came out real funny because the phone was hooked up to a speaker system like we used to have overseas and it let the world in on the know.

Elaine came back so sharp and quick it was like she was trying to bite him. "One of the kids from Ellison just went down."

"So let the Air Force take care of their own. They're autonomous now."

Without being asked to, all the talk came to a standstill. It was as if they were waiting for the bomb to drop, not knowing whether to stay there or run for it.

"Listen, you knothead," she said, "look at the wings you're wearing."

Everybody there looked down at his own chest.

"Those wings he's got on are the same as yours even if they are a whole generation younger. He's one of your own. Do you understand that?"

"Well, what can we . . ."

"He ejected over that damn swamp you playboys call home. He's down right in the middle of it some place and he could possibly be hurt."

"Okay, okay, sugar, but what am I supposed to do?"

"Do? *Do something!* You've been fighting that war so long the only thing you have out there are heroes and you ought to be able to think of something. You're officers, aren't you? You're enlisted specialists, aren't you? Maybe you can take that damn crate of yours and . . ."

"All right, baby, hold it there. You're coming over loud and clear only don't run the old girl down. Where are you?"

"At Ellison with the boy's wife. They live next door to me."

"Where at Ellison?"

"On the flight line," the speaker said. Her voice was flatter now.

"Okay, baby, now calm down. Is there any way there you can contact base ops?"

"I'll find a way."

"Good, then you call from there and by then we'll have something ready."

She hung the phone up almost before he finished and when we looked around it was like looking at the bunch about to hit Ploesti. For a moment the heroes were gone and they were butchers, bakers, and candlestick makers again, slightly paunchy, a lot balder, a little bewildered from being civilians so long. And then Vern spoke.

"Gentlemen," he said. That was all. They all edged in close and the heroes were back once more. They wore the damnedest grins yon ever did see and every hat went over at a jauntier angle and they were ready. *And I mean ready.*

"We're in a peculiar position here. I dare say we are the only ones alive who know that swamp area. It's relatively new, so there are no old timers on it."

I heard Jonesy laugh and say, "Hell, I made a lot of dawn patrols after bass, man."

"I know," Vern told him, "but there's no moon tonight."

Henry Lucerne, our old navigator, said, "We'll go, bucky. Just hand us the poop from group."

Right then the phone rang. Elaine got her message across fast because she had literally busted into ops and the C.O. was on her back. We could hear him squawking over the speaker and then Pappy Thompson, who managed the big A & P store and who had been a general during the war—with the kind of a voice a general should have—reached for the phone and told Vern, "I'll take it."

When he told Elaine to put the C.O. on the guy came on strong until old Pappy said, "This is General Thompson from the Four Hundred and Thirteenth."

Now the 413th went out with the war, but that C.O. didn't know that and he wasn't about to argue with a general.

Pappy said, "What equipment have you there? Any choppers?"

"Er, yes, Sir. Just one, but she's redlined."

"Well dammit, you un-redline it and get it ready. I'll give you thirty minutes to have it on the ramp. You got that?"

"Yessir, yessir," the C.O. stammered uncertainly. "But Sir, where are you?"

"With my men, in the swamp where that boy went down, that's where. Now you get every available man ready. Stand by on an open line and that girl there can pass the messages to you. I want you to relay them directly. Do you hear? Directly. I want no misunderstanding. No garbled orders. Is that clear?"

Well the message went across, all right. You could hear that C.O. sounding off on the other end of that line and now it was up to us. Nobody bothered to change clothes. The flat-boats the sportsmen used were all drawn up at the edge of the water and in five minutes were loaded with gear.

They went out three and four to a boat, some paddling and some with trolling motors. Up front would be one man with a light and another standing by with a boathook to fend off anything from low hanging branches to cottonmouths.

Vern gave a list of things to Pappy and he called them out to Elaine. Ambulance, medics, ropes, power saws, and a dozen other things. She'd relay them across the room and the C.O. would repeat the list.

On the other side of the room the radio that had been drowned out in the chatter was heard again, and this time it was a special bulletin. Nobody could figure it out, but with usual Air Force efficiency an entire rescue team led personally by a general himself was down in the swamps already searching for the lost flier.

We grinned at that, but a sad grin, because we all knew that in a way it was the end of us.

But how that Elaine and Vern did act as a team! You'd think they had been practicing for this all their lives. We sent Curly Mason and Harry Stamph out to direct the crash crews coming in, because without a guide they'd never have made it. Even then we had to use a dozen more to line the road ahead of them so they could pick out the mat under their headlights. Long ago grass had grown through the perforations in the steel and you could hardly tell roadbed from swamp.

You know, it must have been funny to those Air Force boys. Like having a dream. There we'd be, officers and enlisted personnel side by side working hand in glove, decked out in uniforms that disappeared years back. Something like suddenly finding yourself in a lost world.

The fly boys who came in on the crash trucks let their mouths hang open when they dug our 50-mission crushes and the medals that backed our wings up under the lapels almost. But it didn't last long. The mud and sweat made everybody look alike pretty soon.

A little after eleven, Jonesy found the boy near his favorite bass hole. He was hanging from a tree snarled in his shroud lines. Jonesy couldn't tell if he were dead or alive. Everyone was quiet then, until Charlie and Ed got there with another light and Charlie saw the boy move. There was one hell of a shout for pure joy after that.

Then Charlie gave us the bad news. You couldn't make the rescue with a few flashlights and the crash teams had nothing to be used right then. It would take a couple hours to rig something up.

It had to happen. You just know it had to happen.

In fact, I think she was there just waiting for it to happen all along.

We told Charlie to hold it a minute and got the Air Force kids to open hangar doors we never thought would ever be opened again. Then, after Vern told Elaine, "Hold it a minute, baby, because you're going to hear the sweetest love song ever sung," the two of us got aboard the *Dragon Lady* and went through the checklist, and when I said, "Start One," Vern hit the switch.

138

Yessir, she sure did croon. On all four big ones she sang to us, then we opened her eyes wide when we turned on the landing lights and she brightened up the whole swamp.

Oh, how their faces did look when they saw our lady roll out. I guess it was like seeing a live dinosaur to them, because most didn't want to believe it at all. Right then the *Lady* was a living, fire-breathing doll working at what she knew best, taking care of her men, and she was going to make this her last and her biggest.

There were a few of that gang who weren't that young and from up in the cockpit I saw them take a hasty swipe at eyes that turned misty all of a sudden and I knew that she was their lady too as much as she was ours.

Vern went back to the phone and Pappy got the tail jacked up and somehow they were able to swivel our girl around so that midnight was turned into noon, and all the while those four big engines turned generators by whose light a life was being saved.

They got out there with the power saws, cut their way through to the kid in the tree, roped the debris back with winches filled up along the shore, but it wasn't quite enough.

It took the chopper to get him out. Vern directed him in, then Charlie Cross and Ed got the kid in a sling along with a medic who got out there and like it all started . . . suddenly . . . it was all over. Almost, anyway. We put the *Lady* back to sleep, but she wasn't quite the same. She was mired to her belly in the muck of the swamp but we all kissed her tenderly, even those pink-faced Air Force kids, and the two older guys who did it rather forcefully and seemed reluctant to leave her, then we all went to the hangar to smash the glasses in the fireplace. The war was over.

Well, that's when that *Life* photographer found us. Don't ask me how he got there, but he had popped pictures all over the place and there we were, two generations apart, drinking to the old girl outside. Yeah, it made quite a story, our secret society of B-17 lovers who had some harmless good times like it was still a long time ago.

And, of course, now we had to let the girls in, but you can believe it's no sewing circle setup because this is a man's club where all you have to do to get rid of the women is schedule a sex lecture. They don't act up, though. They're all the better for it. Let them get raunchy and you just wave a finger at the beautiful doll under colored lights in the background. You don't buck the *Dragon Lady* in her own house.

Oh, didn't I tell you? That new Air Force over at Ellison threw us a thank-you party and got our lady back out of the muck and into a hangar whose interior *really* is decorated with some of the most beautiful "salvage" you ever saw.

Vern? Shucks, he and Elaine got married and here's the kicker. They did the bit right in the hangar and I was the best man and when she came down the aisle beside the *Dragon Lady* he almost keeled over with surprise because instead of a wedding gown she was wearing the same thing she wore in '41, the pinks and greens of an Army nurse and she was a rank over old Vern.

First thing he did after the ceremony was make old Pappy promote him so he could give her orders. Then he turned and winked at the *Dragon Lady*.

And I'll be hanged if she didn't wink back!

The Dread Chinatown Man

The other day I was walking down Sixth Avenue in New York and directly ahead I spotted a frighteningly familiar face. It was a lot older now, the frame it set on a little stooped, much thinner, but the same face that made my guts churn every time I saw it. So, I did the same thing I used to do a long time ago. Since there was no crowd to get lost in, I stopped, walked back a block and crossed the street to safety where he couldn't get at me. He had on a faded, dingy uniform, but he wasn't military. He didn't own a thing, but the corner was his. Eight million people in New York, but he could pick you out of the mob in a millisecond without goofing once, except in my case . . . and I hated to have to shatter that stupendous ego again . . . even after being made to look like an idiot a dozen times.

You see, he was the Chinatown Man. He was the advance agent for a sightseeing bus to the Mott and Pell Street section and he had a big card above the visor of his cap that read *CHINATOWN TOUR* and made him took like that old conductor on the Toonerville Trolly. He could spot a tourist six blocks off, wait for him to hit the corner, then hassle him into a buck-and-a-half trip so fast the poor yokel never knew what hit him and there was no way his country training could protect him against the big city con the Chinatown Man could pitch.

141

Of course, no self-respecting New Yorker would ever buy the scam, far less than being tabbed for a hayseed. The true natives could handle that with one icy glare or a few choice epithets in a foreign tongue that had plenty of tonal muscle even if he didn't understand it. But he rarely ever heard it because, psychologist that he was, hayseed picking was his specialty.

Now in the old days, I had an office on 45th Street, three blocks away from his outpost. I was a busy little executive in Howard or Crawford suits. I didn't wear white socks and my shoes all came from Thom McAn's. A copy of the *World Telegram* was always under my arm and a faint five o'clock shadow made me look like I had suffered a hard day at work. In other words, I was the typical New Yorker's Brooklynite headed for the Brighton Beach B.M.T. and a pot roast supper.

But not to the Chinatown Man. Oh, no, never to the hayseed picker. I could feel his eyes grab me the minute I turned the corner, keeping me locked in on his mental radar until I got within striking distance; then, out of that whole throng, he'd zero in on me with his pitch and brochure, ticket held at ready and left hand at his change holder on his belt. The spiel was hard, fast and loud with everybody listening in, watching my face get red while I fought him off and if I dropped the *World Telegram* I didn't ever stop to pick it up.

How I got to hate that guy! Every damn night! I couldn't even cross the street without feeling I had lost some of my dignity. All I could do was try to outwit him and look forward to holidays and Thursdays when the shopping crowd gave me enough cover to get by on an end run behind a swarm of blocking backs. Or grin evilly when he was already engaged with a real hayseed and had to let a prospective customer slip out of his grasp.

Then the final insult at me . . . the glove across the jowl, the chip knocked off the shoulder.

I had gone to college at Fort Hays, Kansas, and four of my fraternity brothers came east to visit me. Now, I don't want to finger them as hayseeds, because in *their* backyard a city boy was an absolute misjudgment of nature, but they *did* leave their shoes on the north side of the bed; flush toilets were political necessities and Sears Roebuck was the Neiman Marcus of the area, or even better because the catalog held a dual purpose. They marveled at my white sweater since nobody ever wore anything except maroon or navy blue and at the one BIG *formal* school bash they wondered what that shiny stripe was going down my 'tux' pants and how come I wasn't wearing brown shoes like everybody else? You see, *there* I was the outsider . . . now they were here and we were all walking down Sixth Avenue after I had given them a big taste of the big city, Automat for breakfast, chop suey for lunch, early show at the Apollo Burlesque, where Georgia Southern flipped them out, and a quick run-through of the office where we put comic books together.

Big city brother had the country cousins in tow, enjoying having them on his own turf for a change, proving that we had garages bigger than the hotel in Hays, 20-chair barber shops and more taxis than Kansas had cars. They marveled at my dollar tips, the speed of the express elevators in the Empire State Building and interpreted New Yorkese for them in the Stage Door Deli.

Oh, I was big, all right, but I never should have brought them back to 45th Street to see the office. I had forgotten that the Chinatown Man would be waiting. But when I remembered it was too late—until I looked at the Kansas Kids. They were the best cover I ever had. This time he'd have to draw the line smack down the middle once and for

143

all, and after that I'd be home free.

I guess you know what the lousy slob did.

All of a sudden those watery blue eyes picked up their target right in front of the Big Man's audience, grabbed my sleeve and started his pitch. Only this time I didn't drop the *World Telegram*. The Gotham gambit hit me with the secondary move and I looked the Chinatown Man straight in the peepers with a Times Square snarl and said, "Look, I was born in New York, I lived here and I already been to Chinatown 20 times and if I go there I don't take no sightseein' bus. You unnerstan'?"

He reeled, he choked . . . and as the literary types say, he was aghast. My fraternity brothers were real proud of me, but wondered what had happened to my language. They hardly understood it at all. The Chinatown Man's eyes were a little misty.

The next day the guys went back to Kansas. I went back to work. I came out of the office at a quarter after five and headed for the subway. I almost made it. The enemy I had thought was dead wasn't dead at all. The bastard had bailed out and all of a sudden he was coming at me again. The hand grabbed my sleeve, the brochure and ticket was shoved in my face and I said, "Look I told you yesterday . . ."

"Oh," he told me with casual reluctance, "It's you."

Now here it is 30 years later. I'm walking up Sixth Avenue going north. Wars have been fought, tycoons have been battled and beaten, books, movies and TV have made you famous and people say hello on the street. The suit is custom made. You're a big boy, buddy, so march on . . . everybody knows you.

But, like I said, there are some battles you never can win, so I withdraw, walked back a block, crossed the street and flagged me down a cab.

I still couldn't face the Chinatown Man.

Toys for the Man-Child

I was beginning to think that I was the only grown-up who likes to play with toys. Not the sophisticated power-driven goodies and stuff . . . but just plain old toys that could Walter Mitty you into a happy fantasy land where adventure runs wild and nobody really gets hurt at all.

Then the other day I was prowling through this four-storied hobby shop trying to look like I didn't belong there, ostensibly on a search to "bring home something for the kid," but knowing right where I was going, and picking up two kits of a new plastic glider job with fantastic aerodynamic capabilities. The other one was, of course, in case the first one got broken, despite the manufacturer's claims of nearly total indestructibility.

Hell, that other one was for me. I wasn't about to let a six-year-old kid have all the fun, especially when I saw the ad first. I don't think the salesman bought my line. He had probably been through it before and just played it cool, but the well-dressed guy next to me who had been flying the miniature chopper, hand-operated through an egg-beater drive and flexible cable, gave me a silly grin because he had a pair of them and the same explanation that I had.

And there we were, trapped. Two grown men who should have known better. He finally said, "You too?" I nodded. He gave me a silly grin. "I have a sailboat too—I keep it in the pool."

"So have I. My wife bought it for me."

"How'd it go?"

"Great . . . now. When I got the thing it had plastic sails that didn't work so I got hold of some fabric and a grommet punch and fitted it out right."

"The kid like it?" he asked suspiciously.

"Hell, I don't let him near it. He can watch, but don't touch."

And so began a very profitable business acquaintanceship nurtured on a quiet pond or an open field and sometimes on the top of the playroom bar that makes a great racetrack and a handy place to talk over new modifications and results.

Like the wives say, it's cheaper than golf, less wearing on the heart and it keeps them at home. But why the heck can't they put their junk away when they're done? And who made these scratches on the table?

So when I happened to be at the Murrell's Inlett Art and Crafts Festival and stumbled into the handmade toy area, I knew I didn't have to feel like a loner anymore. It was like something right out of the good old days with Dancing Darts, climbing monkeys, whip tops, tongue-depressor and Popsickle stick fliers, rubber-band guns and all the props we thought we had invented as kids, but had really been handed down through the generations . . . until this one.

What was really funny . . . the kids couldn't work them, but the old men sure knew how to do it and for the first time there was that light of total amazement in a boy's face when big daddy-o made those gadgets go.

Oh, a few things have changed and you can see why the kids were done out of some of the fun we had because of modern technology. The old snappy rubber inner tubes we used to cut up to make those great guns that could sting the parts of a girl's legs that showed under her bloomers had been replaced by butyl with no snap at all. But the same technology came up with surgical rubber that really put a zing in them. Now you can pick a fly off the wall at 30 feet and make your sister yelp like a loon right through her mini-skirt.

Seems like the women don't sew much anymore, so you don't collect a box full of empty thread spools to notch up and rubber-band power into mock tanks on rainy days anymore. Unless you uncover a forgotten button box with those big, ivory two-holers, you have to invent a replacement friction clutch, and between Zippo and Ronson, wooden stick matches are obsolete, so the rigged shaft drive of the "tank" becomes a plastic substitute. But they don't quite work as well as the old ones did . . . and to listen to that older generation explain the relative merits of the kind *they* had was something else again.

The guy who had spent a winter collecting the obsolete essentials and tooling them up for his nostalgic display of the before-battery era had a run on his supplies he couldn't believe. Unlike his kid, the old man knew those tongue-depressor propellers you whipped out between your palms always seemed to get hung up in the front yard tree, so he didn't buy just one . . . he bought a bagful and screw the tree. The wind always got them down later and why risk a broken leg for just one? And it took more than one tank to fight a battle, so another bagful. Somebody was always breaking the Dancing Dan board, so you got spares, and just so there could be a duet, another Dancing Dan went into the sack too. On top, throw a couple of climbing monkeys, a whip top, two rubber guns because retaliation is always necessary if you want a happy home . . .

Now, the guy who did all this thought he had run the

gamut of "what the kids used to play with," but he didn't know the half of it. The next day a bunch of his customers showed up with their own pet versions of rubber-band-motored, mothball-powered shingle boats, four-shot, rapid-fire inner-tube rifles and my contribution of a Crisco-can cannon that fired when a mixture of spit and carbide crystals generated enough gas to touch off at a nail hole with a wooden match. Frankly, that one was the hit of the show even if it did scare hell out of the mothers and it might even set off a new run on shortening tins. The only trouble is, those new plastic lids don't last very long. Nothing like the good old tin tops back in the pre-plastic days.

All the way across the country I had a good top pal and I couldn't let him be forgotten—I picked up two of each of the ready-made from the crafts man, packaged a bag of carbide crystals into an empty Crisco can with four extra covers and (nail hole installed), typed out the instructions with a Band-Aid stapled to the top to indicate caution and headed for the post office with my package. He could use his own spit.

The other day his wife told me he's had her on a pie baking spree and I didn't have the heart to tell her it was one way to get Crisco cans without looking silly. Besides, she's a little worried about him. Seems like he's always poking into her sewing kit and she's finding balled up handfuls of discarded thread around and he's got a new lock on a closet behind the playroom bar.

One other thing. We just signed a new contract without any negotiations at all. We had to get on with the game.

Hot Cat

She's lying quietly out there on the bottom now—melted, frag-
mented pieces of metal scattered like dust across the sand,
nameless, traceless, but evoking a memory that could make you
sweat cold if you knew the truth about her.

Not too far away is another mass of metal, twisted and cor-
roded by now, but still recognizable for what it was. Both
masses had been born together and served together, then sep-
arated for 20 years to meet again in a fusion of terror that was,
fortunately, almost totally, unseen.

There was still one other memory . . . a sudden, bright-
red, misty memory better forgotten.

Chapter 1

I sat there with the half-finished coffee in my hand, watching
them service the battered old Mustang on the runway outside.
There was nothing of interest there; I had seen it done too many
times before. But the blonde reflected in the plate glass window
of the bar *was* interesting, especially when she knew I was
watching her and arranged herself so I could see her legs from
the best angle.

Step one in the big play, I thought. She was chumming for

149

me and next would come the hook. Cute, real cute, I looked like something out of the "Late Show" in an old AAF A-2 jacket with a leather helmet and goggles jammed into my pocket, and she was a dream in a fitted covert suit that made her hair look like a summer sunset.

The trouble was, I knew her, only she didn't know me. Three years ago, Lois Hays had interviewed me in a German hospital to find out why I was interested in making an air drop of ammo into Hungary from an old Ju-88. I could have told her it was for the loot, but my face was bandaged and still hurt from the shrapnel slice so I didn't bother. That time she had played the part in a nurse's outfit.

Dominick Lolla, who got me smuggled back to the States on a tramp steamer, knew her, too. He was an accredited *Circut* correspondent and didn't hold much with anybody doing legwork for Duncan Knight, whose "Washington Inside" column was dedicated to ripping apart our military policy.

I grinned at her reflection. *So what the hell, if you need legwork done, get someone with pretty legs to do it.* Hers were beautifully rounded and shiny with nylon until the sheen stopped and there was a quick flash of tan before she pulled the hem of her skirt down.

And when you're looking at legs you don't see people, so when the big guy said, "Mr. Fallon?" it caught me by surprise.

He had an angular face, almost devoid of expression, but ready to be friendly if he had to. His suit was well cut, but not new, and fitted with some peculiar purpose in mind. The smaller man with him was on the mouse side, with an irritated squint to his eyes.

I stood up. "Cop?"

"Lieutenant Trusky, city police." He held out his hand.

"It shows?" His voice sounded amused.

His hand was hard. "To some."

"This is Mr. Del Reed from the state's attorney's office."

The smaller guy nodded curtly and shifted his briefcase. "If you have a few minutes I'd like to talk to you," he said.

"What about?"

"You have a few minutes?" Trusky asked politely.

"Sure."

"Then let's find out."

Behind me the blonde uncrossed those legs again and watched us. Del Reed nodded toward the small restaurant section, across the room, and when Trusky moved up beside me I could feel the gun at his hip.

"How long did you know Tucker Stacy, Mr. Fallon?"

Del Reed didn't waste any time with pleasantries. "Since 'forty-two," I said. "We were in the Army together. Air Force cadets."

"You were in the same outfit together. Two hundred-fifty-second Fighter Squadron, I believe."

"If you know so damn much, why the questions?"

Reed's face tightened, but a wave from Lieutenant Trusky calmed him down. "All right, let's get to the point," he said. He pulled a folder from his briefcase, held it in his lap and fingered the contents. "You and Stacy were discharged together, shared a brief business venture . . ."

"Crop-dusting," I interrupted. "We went broke."

". . . Corresponded a few times and except for a squadron reunion in nineteen fifty-four, apparently never had any further contact." His eyes left the folder and drifted up to meet mine.

"So what?" I said.

"So out of a clear blue sky he left you a half-million dollar investment."

151

I put down my coffee and leaned on the table. The little man was getting to me.

"Is his family contesting his will?" I asked.

Reed's mouth twitched. "You know he has none."

"Is the state?"

"Well, no."

"Don't hesitate, Mr. Reed. You're off limits and you know it. Put it on the line or take a walk. You just don't impress me at all."

"Del is trying to . . . let's say, forestall action, Mr. Fallon," Trusky said quietly.

"The will hasn't even been probated yet," I reminded him. "I'm here because Tuck's lawyer wrote me. Now where does the state come in? So Tuck leaves his old buddy an airfield, the Capital K. I come down here to see what it's all about and the action starts before I even get there."

"Had you known about the will?" Reed said.

"No. But it doesn't surprise me."

"Why not?"

"Because we're two of a kind. Neither one of us had anybody else. In the Army we took pretty good care of each other, and if one of us had been knocked off the other would have gotten his gear."

"Who was your National Service Insurance made out to, Mr. Fallon?"

"An orphanage, Mr. Reed. So was Tuck's. If you read all those papers you should know that."

He ignored the remark. "Do you have a will?"

"What for? Outside of that Mustang, I don't have anything."

Trusky tapped the table with a forefinger. "Old fighter plane, isn't it?"

"You know it. You were there, weren't you?"

The cop smiled and shrugged. "Practical to own?"

"For my purposes," I told him.

Reed snapped the folder shut. "And what may those purposes be?"

I pointed toward his lap. "What do the papers say, buddy?"

"That you worked for a motion picture company. I can't see where owning an airplane . . ."

"You don't see much at all. Were you elected or appointed?"

"Appointed, but . . ."

"Then somebody's pretty damn stupid."

"Listen!"

"Aw, shut up." I looked at Trusky and he was trying not to grin. I said, "I've worked with Demeret Pictures off and on for ten years. When they go on location, I fly the daily takes back to the lab for developing, then hustle them up to the location for screening the next day. But that's beside the point. Let's get to the business you're trying to involve me in."

Trusky said, "If you inherit the Capital K, what do you intend doing with it?"

"Run it . . . sell it . . . how the hell do I know. You got any ideas?"

"I might."

"Then let's hear them."

"Let's see what you do with it first."

It started to come through then, even the bit with the blonde outside. "What was Tucker doing with it?" I asked them.

Trusky threw Reed a sidewards glance and when the attorney nodded he said, "There's been some speculation in higher quarters that your friend might have been engaged in some illegal activities."

"Like what?"

He shrugged again. "Florida's close to enough places to make a lot of illegal things practical if you don't mind getting killed for them." They stood up and Trusky said, "See you tomorrow. We're going through all of your friend's papers, private and business. Everything. You can lodge a complaint if you feel like it."

I gave him a grin that was all teeth. "Hell, why should I? Be my guest."

Chapter 2

The wire services had never said much about it. Tucker had simply flown out in the Staggerwing Beech he had liked so well and never come back. He had told Charlie Traub, his chief mechanic, that he was going to do some preliminary work on an aerial survey job he was bidding on and headed for the southern tip of Florida. An hour after take-off, a line squall came up. It was supposed that Tuck tried to fly around it, couldn't get through and ditched in the ocean. An air-sea rescue unit located pieces of wreckage that were unmistakably from his plane.

You get old but never bold. It just didn't sound like Tuck.

Only the local paper played up the incident big. Tucker Stacy was a prominent character in Celada, a war hero who turned an old Air Force auxiliary field into the Capital K and promoted a couple of electronics plants to locate in the area. That, with a booming resort section, put Celada on the map and Tucker Stacy in the city council.

Old Tuck, how he had changed. He sure used to be the wild-assed one, ready to charge into anything. Nine confirmed kills on Me-109s. Tuck? Hey, remember that leave in

London? That pair of Scot lassies! Crazy, man. What did they teach them on that farm? Remember? *Remember, hell. When you're dead you don't remember anything.*

I propped the scuffed jump boots on the end of the couch and looked at the ceiling. Across the room, the TV was giving the weather reports for tomorrow. Hot. Clear. Probably local thundershowers in the afternoon.

When the knock came I said, "Come on in," and didn't take my eyes off the ceiling. The door *snicked* shut. "I've been waiting for you," I said.

Lois Hays tilted her head and smiled. "Sure of yourself, aren't you?"

"Why not?"

She was prettier face to face than reflected in a plate glass window. Even though the suit was cut in an almost military fashion, she couldn't hide the full thrust of her breasts or the rich sweep of her hips and thighs.

"You got pretty legs," I said. "Pneumatic. Soft, cushiony."

"I don't know if I should thank you or not."

"Never mind that. Just make the pitch."

"What?"

"Honey," I said, "you made the point clear in the lounge. I dug the bit with the legs and all. I appreciate the generosity. Now let's hear the offer."

For a moment she poised there, motionless, then her face flushed and the anger tightened her mouth. But only for a second. The pink left her cheeks and she laughed deep in her throat. "I think you've known too many hotel rooms and too many . . ."

"Whores?" I added for her.

She didn't get mad. "Like you say, why not?"

I turned my head and grinned. I couldn't have made a

pretty sight. I still hadn't shaved and the scar on my face always showed worse then. "Wrong, baby. I'm a funny sort of guy. I never buy it. It gets given to me or I take it."

"Should I be frightened?" She laughed again and sat down.

"Not tonight, kid. I'm tired. It's been a long day." I closed my eyes and settled back. "What do you want?"

"A story."

"Yeah, sure."

I could feel her smiling. "My name is Karen Morgan. I'm with Barrett Syndicated Features and I'd like to get some background on Tucker Stacy, and, of course, you and your plans. You may not know it, but Mr. Stacy's activities were of great interest statewide."

"Honey," I said, "cut the crap."

I opened my eyes and she was watching me, the softness gone from her face. She was steady, studying me, waiting. "I don't understand," she said.

"Tuck's death is only a local matter," I said.

Her tongue touched her lips. "All right, I'll come clean," she said. "There's been speculation."

"How about that."

"Aren't you interested?"

"Kid, Tuck and I faced death plenty of times. You're bound to get it someday anyway. I've had a plane torn apart under me in a storm."

"Have you checked the weather for the day he died? Several planes flew through that line squall without any difficulty."

"Sugar, inside a thunderhead . . ."

"There weren't any severe ones. I have verified pilot reports to that effect. So does Miami. The squall line was light. A Cessna 90 and two Tripacers passed through it."

"So?"

"So there's been some speculation . . ."

I twisted on the couch and propped my head in my hand. "What about?"

Her smile was almost disarming. "Were you ever a policeman?"

"No, but I've operated in their area of work."

"Very well. Mr. Stacy, it was rumored, was not above turning a dishonest dollar."

"With all his loot and his investment here it doesn't sound reasonable, honey. As an airport, the Capital K is a going concern. Try again."

She stood up quickly, frowning in concentration, and walked toward me. There was a "woman-with-a-mission" look spread right across her face. "A few years ago he had nothing except a few surplus airplanes. Somehow he managed all this. It came suddenly and expanded fast. The big question is why."

"He was lucky, baby."

"All right. Then the big question is *how*."

I shrugged. Tuck's business was no affair of mine. "Where do I come in?"

She found my eyes with hers. "Supposing he did have an illegal operation going somewhere, then the possibility of his having been killed would be increased, correct?"

I nodded noncommittally.

"And there's a possibility that he would have left some record of a sort."

I nodded again.

"If I could see his papers . . . or whatever effects he left . . . I might be able to come up with a story." She paused and gave an impatient toss of her head. Hair swirled across her shoulders like a golden wave. "You inherit his property. You could let me do this. Will you?"

157

"Maybe," I said. "What'll you give me?"

Her eyebrows raised. "What . . . do you want?"

"Try me and see."

For three full seconds she stood there, a curious smile toying with the edges of her mouth. Then her hands went to the buttons of her jacket and flipped them open. She dropped it to the floor, then did the same thing to her blouse. There was another minute pause before her fingers went to the hooks of the brassiere at her back. With a motion of her shoulders, she let it slip down her arms, dangled it a moment in her fingers, then dropped that, too.

The smile was gone now. In its place there was an intense, sultry look she couldn't conceal. Her breasts were magnificently full, seeming to pulsate with pressure that wanted to burst through the taut red nipples. Her breath was jerky and a shudder went through her shoulders to twist down into the supple, trim waist that flowed into her skirt.

I hadn't moved. I just watched her. It was something she had never done before and showed it, and the doing had turned her into a person she had tried hard to conceal. She swayed toward me and in another moment would have taken the step that would put her inside my reach. Already I could see her hand groping, feeling for the zipper at her side.

I got up quickly, walked to the door and turned around. "Nice act, Lois, but you'll never make the big time."

It was as if I had belted her. The longing disappeared and for a moment there was a hint of fear, then something else.

"*Lois?*" she said.

"We've met before, baby. You didn't get what you came after then, either."

Chapter 3

From the air the runway system of Tuck's airport was shaped
like a capital K, and that's how it got its name. It was built
during the war as an auxiliary to nearby Martin AAFB, but not
enough B-24s or 17s put down there to cave in the runways so it
was in top shape. Tuck had erected a fine operations building,
attached a lounge and restaurant, added a motel unit and a
group of specialty shops built around a generous swimming
pool. There was a golf course bordering the south edge of the
field, several tennis courts, an adjacent highway and, at the far
end of the field, away from the social center, the hangar area.
Not a very military setup, but a profitable deal in these days of
fly-in vacations. At night, each burning light read like a dollar
sign. The motel units were filled, maintenance and repair was
going on around the clock in the hangars, and overhead was the
sporadic drone of light planes coming into the pattern.

At 9 o'clock I got one of the kids who drove the caddy cars
to take me to the hangars. Tuck had had his office there,
where he liked it best . . . in the middle of engines and air-
frames. Sam Devin, Tuck's attorney, would have preferred
his own office, but he was looking to please what might mean
a new account, so he came where I asked him to.

Sam was a short, wiry guy with a grey crew-cut. He was
probably pushing sixty but moved like thirty. His eyes gave
him away. They had seen the inside of too many courtrooms
and too much misery. We shook hands briefly, and Sam said,
"Charlie Traub will be here in just a minute. Mind waiting?"

I said no, poured myself a beer from the cooler in the
corner and sat down. Charlie Traub came in like a little fox
terrier, introduced himself to me on the way to the cooler and
pulled up a chair.

In one way he was like Sam. He had the stamp of the old-time flier all over him, from his stained white coveralls to the wrench scars on his knuckles. They were both about the same age until you read their eyes. There was still a lot of life left in Charlie's.

Sam spread his papers out on the desk. "Ready?"

Both of us nodded.

"Fine." He picked up the top sheet, glanced at it briefly and put it down. "Tucker's will provides for two persons. Charlie Traub here gets twenty thousand in cash, three airplanes specified here and a five percent participation in the profits of the Capital K. He is to remain here in his present position for one year before he can be fired."

"And to Cat Fallon here goes the entire rest of Tucker's estate. I haven't had time to itemize the assets, but to give you an idea, I'd say the cash value of his properties is about a million. On deposit is some two hundred thousand dollars."

"Anything else?" I asked.

"Just a personal letter to you, Mr. Fallon." Sam fingered an envelope and handed it across the desk to me. It was sealed and the note inside was undated. From what it said, it seemed neither important nor cryptic.

Dear Cat: Keep things going for me. There aren't too many of us left. A few maybe, but not many. Like Verdo and Cristy. Have fun. Don't choke on a banana.

I felt myself frowning at the note the second time I read it. Who the hell were Verdo and Cristy? The names sounded familiar enough, but I sure couldn't recall them. Back in the old days, Tuck knew everybody on the base and in town. Me, I didn't give a damn for any of them. Verdo and Cristy! Well, hello to them wherever they were. I folded the note and stuck it in my pocket.

Sam said, "Now for your immediate plans, Mr. Fallon . . ."

I waved him off. "Let's keep things running the way they are. Charlie knows the maintenance end and the rest of the staff must be on the ball. The Capital K has been making money. I'll take a look at Tuck's personal end and see how I can fit in. Hell, I got no place else to go anyway. Sound okay?"

"Fine with me," Charlie mused.

Sam stood up and began collecting his papers. "I'll have everything in final form in a few days," he said.

"Before you go," I said, "just one more thing. Between us."

Both of them glanced up sharply.

"Did Tuck have something going for him?"

They exchanged sharp looks, then Charlie squinted and looked at the ceiling. "Like what, Cat?"

"Let's cut it clean. Was he involved in anything illegal?"

"Why do you ask?"

"Because, Sam, the cops are already asking questions and I gave my approval for them to poke around Tuck's papers. How does that sound to you? Upset any applecarts?"

He didn't hesitate. "Nope. They can look all they want. If Tuck or anybody else were involved with an illegal operation to my knowledge . . . or even if I suspected it . . . I wouldn't be here."

"Good enough. How about you, Charlie?"

"As far as I know, nix. He made some smart deals, but legal right down the line. He never chiseled or stole and his credit was tops. He's flown out of here alone many a time without bothering to tell me where he was headed. I didn't check his flight plans or even know if he filed any. But hell, a guy's entitled to some time off. So maybe he went to Vegas or to one of those fancy fly-in fields where they have a cathouse at the end of a runway. Okay?"

I thought it over and nodded. "Suits me. I just don't want my neck stuck out."

"You're the boss now," Charlie said. "Any orders?"

"Yeah. Fix me up with one of the motel units. I'll have my stuff sent over from the hotel. And run a hundred-hour check on the Mustang."

"No trouble. What about parts?"

"Trans-Florida Aviation over in Sarasota has a full stock of P-Fifty-One components. And since we have some loot in the bank, don't go scrimping. My instrument panel is out-dated, so get the King Radio catalogue and mount me up. I want new tires and canopy on the baby and find a reticule for the gunsight."

"You got a K-fourteen on that thing?"

"Uh-huh."

"What for? You can bust your head if you . . ."

"I always wear the shoulder harness locked on landing, buddy. Besides, I might want to shoot somebody."

"Oh," he grinned, "a nostalgic."

"There aren't too many of us left," I said. Then I remembered it was what Tuck had written. I tried to remember who Verdo and Cristy were. There was some reason why I should remember them, but the reason was twenty years old and only a hazy recollection now.

The kind of circles I traveled in made it no trouble to en-large my contacts. One call to Slim Upgate in New York put me through to a lead man in Celada named George Clinton, and with a clearance like Upgate he was glad to give me a run down on Tucker Stacy. Briefly, he told me, Tuck was a wheeler-dealer who operated on a comparatively small scale, liked what he had in Celada and decided to stick around. Clinton hinted that Tuck had some outside interests, but speculated that they lay somewhere between a man's normal attachments for girls and gambling. He didn't think it was anything in the rackets.

When I mentioned the cops, Clinton shrugged, but Del Reed's name brought a squint to his eyes and he made a couple of phone calls. After the last one he hung up, dragged on a cigar and told me Del Reed was the state man handling any of the operations involving the new Cuban setup, especially the anti-Cuban bunch in the Miami area.

"Where would Tuck fit into that picture?"

"I could guess," Clinton said.

"Then guess."

"He had planes, an airfield. Now you guess."

"Smuggling?" Clinton made a vague gesture. "No, that's not logical," I continued. "He couldn't get into Cuba to start with. Besides, they come out in bunches. They commandeer boats generally."

"The big ones?"

"Aren't most of the big ones already here?"

Clinton studied his cigar a moment. "Yes, I'd say so." He looked up at me. "There's still a bunch operating in the mountains like Castro did."

"No dice, friend. Castro's was an army of poorly trained malcontents who were glad to see Batista go. It's not like that now. With Russian and Chinese Commies in there running things, whatever opposition shows its face will get smeared like a bug. The groups in the mountains are scattered little units. Any real opposition to Castro will come right out of the States."

"You never know what the Commies are going to pull," Clinton said. "Well, if there's anything else you want any help with, let me know."

"I will."

"You want me to pull the local fuzz off your neck?"

"That's a real power play, friend."

Clinton made another small gesture with his hands. "I'm a heavy contributor to certain campaign funds. Little favors I can get."

"Save them until we need them."

"Suit yourself," he said.

Out of habit, I checked the weather before I hit the pad. The latest out of Miami had a tropical disturbance building up. The weathermen had already named the hurricane Ingrid. It was enough to put a crimp in the traffic pattern even though the sky was clear and the wind a gentle five knots from the west.

Charlie Traub's crew had already started tearing down the Mustang, and after a cursory look around, I walked back to the end unit of the motel that had been Tuck's, stripped down, took a shower and flaked out on the bed.

For a while I lay there with my hands behind my head, trying to get inside Tuck's mind. Damn, there wasn't one reason in the world outside of sentiment that would have made him leave me all his goodies. Big wheelers just don't have sentiment. I had known too many of them. If I had been an operator who could make a go out of what Tuck had built up, I could see a reason, but I wasn't an operator.

So maybe it *was* sentiment, like that reflection back to Verdo and Cristy. I'd have to look them up, whoever they were. Maybe a couple of late replacements from a repple-depple in '45. Tuck always did baby the new ones. Me, I watched out for me first.

Sentiment? No, there was another reason somewhere. Meanwhile, I had a half million bucks to play with and no sentiment involved. It was going to be a lot of fun. One big ball and to hell with everybody. When it was over and spent, I'd climb back in the rebuilt Mustang and find some more fresh sky to find a buck in.

That's how I fell asleep.

And when I woke up she was standing there in the moonlight with a gun in her hand pointing it at my head. Not a little girl-type rod, but a fat black musket that was a .38 police positive with a four-inch barrel. In the pale yellow glow from outside I could see the dull grey of the slugs in the cylinder.

She was only smaller than average in height. The rest of her was all magnificent woman that slacks and a sweater couldn't hide. Only the total black of her hair lightened her face by contrast. No sun-worshipper could have had a more luxurious tan.

She saw my eyes open. "Don't move, *señor,*" she said.

"I could use a sheet over me."

"I've seen naked men before."

"Drop dead," I said, and flipped the sheet over myself.

"You almost *did,* Mr. Fallon. Don't move again."

I could see the expression on her face, a peculiar set to her eyes. She wasn't fooling. It had been close. Very slowly I settled back and folded my hands behind my head. Never trust a broad with a gun. If she could use it, that made it even worse.

"Your play, baby."

"Quite, Mr. Fallon." Her voice carried a soft Spanish inflection.

"Am I supposed to know you?"

I could see the tip of her tongue wet her lips indecisively. "Not necessarily. I am Sharon Ortiz."

"Cuban?"

She didn't hesitate. "My father was Spanish. We lived in

Cuba. My mother was Irish." Her mouth smiled over beautiful white teeth, but there was no humor there at all. "But I am Cuban, *señor*."

"And what do you want with me?"

"Right now I am to decide whether you would be better dead or alive."

"Great. How does it look?"

Her hand tightened around the .38. I hadn't figured out yet how I was going to take it away from her. "Don't be flippant, Mr. Fallon. This is not a toy."

I gave her words back to her. "I've seen guns before."

"Yes, I imagine you have."

"Then either use it or tell me what the hell you want."

Her eyes never wavered from mine. "You prefer to stay alive?"

"Sure."

"Then you are to stay here, out of sight. You are to see no one, talk to no one. You will give us . . . one other person and myself . . . authorization to inspect all of Tucker Stacy's personal belongings and this entire installation. Then you may live."

"Thanks. Now what are you after?"

"It isn't necessary for you to know."

"Sorry, baby," I said.

She was going to do it, damned if she wasn't. She thumbed the hammer back for single-action release and took one step toward the bed to be certain of her target and that's what happens when you send a girl out to do a man's job. When you shoot somebody you do it *then* and from where you stand. You don't take time to single-action a double-action gun or step into the target where a guy can kick the piece right out of your mitt with one foot and yank you into the sack with the other.

It doesn't take much to turn a tough broad into a soft one. You take all their defenses away when you grab them by the collar and rip the clothes off their back. I hooked my fingers in the waistband of her slacks and with one wrench tore them loose with the pink things underneath. The spitting, clawing tiger became a sobbing, frightened woman in seconds.

She was beautiful, a terrified, beautiful animal with black hair and tawny skin and big, round eyes filled with horror— not so much at what she thought was going to happen to her, but at the mistake she had made.

I said, "You could have caught more flies with honey than with vinegar, baby."

Then, instantly, the woman touch was there again and she saw her out. *Give a little, get a little,* she was thinking.

"But not this time, baby." I grabbed her by the arm, dragged her off the bed and hustled her to the door. I gave her a shove outside where the scream she started broke off into a gasp when she realized she was naked in the world.

I laughed, locked the door and went back inside. I found the .38, stuck it in my pants hanging on the back of a chair and sat on the edge of the bed. She'd be back. You don't do things like that to a broad who comes calling with a gun without her coming back.

Outside, the wind had picked up a little. It felt good rolling across my chest. I pulled the sheet up and went back to sleep grinning.

Hell of a thing. Two of them almost back-to-back, Lois and Sharon. I was throwing away more than most guys ever got.

Chapter 4

At 7:30, I had breakfast and went over to the operations building. Charlie Traub was already there with Del Reed and Lieutenant Trusky. When I nodded to Charlie he came over, both hands jammed in his coverall pockets.

"These clowns been poking around ever since dawn," he said.

"I told them they could."

"Not in my private office. They got two men over there now cleaning up the mess they made. I won't stand for that crap. You know what they're looking for?"

"How would I? Hell, let them look. The sooner they get done the sooner they're out of my hair."

"Sure, but you better talk to Trusky."

"Why?"

"You'll find out."

I told Charlie to get back to the hangars and walked to the files. Everything from them was spread across the counter while Del Reed fingered each sheet carefully.

"Find what you're looking for?" I asked.

Del Reed put down a folder. "Not yet, Mr. Fallon, but we will."

"If Tuck ever went to Cuba, I doubt if he'd file a flight plan."

This time both of them stopped at once and turned toward me. "You seem to know a lot, Mr. Fallon," Del smiled. There was no friendliness there, just the smile of a lawyer baiting a witness.

It took Trusky to break through the ice. "Knock it off, Del. He's played too many of these games." His eyes glued themselves to mine. "Suppose you try talking a little bit, Fallon. Like where your information comes from."

"Back issues of the Miami papers," I lied. "Interesting articles about your partner here and his pet activities . . . the Cuban bit. That's all he touches . . . that's all he's assigned to. Right?"

"Go on."

"So it figures, Lieutenant. Tucker had planes and an airfield. He had an interest in politics. He's suddenly dead and the Cuban expert turns up to go through his records. Now let's tighten things up a little. Let's go into my office where you two can talk to me. If I like what you say, I won't throw up any roadblocks. You're here at my convenience, and I can crowd you out any time I like. Try subpoenaing anything and the story comes out. I don't think you want that just yet. Okay, now what do we do?"

Trusky looked at Reed. The little man glared at me and nodded.

"Clean up the mess first," I said, "then meet me in my office."

Later, over Reed's objections, Trusky laid it out. He said, "You know the background on the Cuban deal. Right now the ticklish part is that anti-Castro people ready for an armed attack are here in Florida. It's something that should be dealt with on a national level, but because of the peculiar circumstances and the proximity of Cuba, it's all centered in the end of one state. Our people have put up with it and are better qualified in most cases to deal with things.

"However, all the anti-Castro bunch aren't Cubans. Plenty of U.S. types are right there with them. We suspect your former buddy Tuck was one of them."

"So what?" I said. "I feel the same way. What's wrong with that?"

Del Reed stood up impatiently. "Wrong? I'll tell you what's wrong. If it's played out politically or economically

169

that's one thing, but when it comes to any acts of violence it could touch off a hot war. Don't you realize the Reds are just waiting for us to make a move so they'll have some excuse to come to the aid of Castro? Don't you think they'd have a beautiful piece of propaganda going for them if one of our citizens got caught up in an international mess?"

Reed leaned on the desk, his face livid. "Tucker Stacy was reported to have made numerous unauthorized flights out of the country. He was reported seen in the company of several well-known anti-Castro people on several occasions."

"Reported," I reminded him, "not proven. And if you *do* prove it, what can you do? He's dead."

"Exactly." His face was bright with sweat now. "And supposing his death was not accidental and it gets out. Do you realize the stink our own people will make? You realize how much closer that can push us to all-out war?"

"Maybe it's about time," I said.

Del rubbed his hands together until he regained his composure. "Don't be stupid. Nobody wins with a war."

"Maybe not, but you could still be doing this wrong."

"Then *you* tell *us*," Trusky said.

"Let it die. No harm is done."

Reed's face showed his contempt for my suggestion. "Unfortunately, the damage might already be done. Tucker Stacy was a brilliant promoter. There's no way of telling how far he went or what was involved. One thing we're sure of. Your friend was in the hottest juggling act that's come up so far. All we know is that something big was underway and he was part of it. We have to know what it was. Do we have your cooperation?"

"Sure," I said, "only you have a time limit. Three days. That ought to be cooperation enough."

"Well?" Trusky asked.

Del Reed nodded. "That will do it."

Before they could leave, there was a rap on the door. It swung open and Charlie Traub poked his head in. "Some broad here for you, Cat."

"Send her in."

The request was almost useless. Lois Hays came sweeping past Charlie before he could ask her. I grinned, waiting to see the malice in her face, but there was none. "Well, hello, sugar," I said. "Meet Mr. Reed and Lieutenant Trusky."

Something happened to Del's face. It seemed to freeze up. "We've met before, Mr. Fallon."

"Yes, in a courtroom, wasn't it?"

"Quite. Now, if you'll excuse us, Mr. Fallon, we'll get on with things." He nodded curtly to Lois, and walked to the door with Trusky behind him. The cop's eyes were half closed, and I could sense his mind working. Halfway out, Reed paused and said over his shoulder, "I can expect a confidence between us, can't I?"

"I wouldn't worry," I told him.

Lois had seated herself behind the desk and was sucking gently on a cigarette. Her eyes were laughing at me now. She answered my question before I could ask it. "No, I'm not mad. In fact, I think you were kind of cute. Anybody else would have gone all the way."

"I've been there, baby, it's nothing new anymore."

"But I'm curious, Mr. Fallon . . ."

"Cat."

"All right. Cat. You said we had met before." She blew a cloud of silver smoke toward me. "Where?"

"Uh-uh. I like my advantage. Maybe some other time I'll tell you. Right now get on with your pitch. What's it this time?"

She waved one hand toward the closed door. "You had an

important visitor. What's he doing here?"

I shrugged and slid off the desk. "The same thing you're doing."

Her eyebrows went up with mock curiosity.

"Come on, quit the games. I wasn't born yesterday, kid. He's a state rep engaged in political work dealing with the Cuban situation. You're a nosy legman for a political reporter. You both want the same thing."

"And what would that be, Cat?"

"Whatever you think Tucker Stacy was doing for the anti-Castro bunch."

"It would make a good story. It *is* my job, you know."

"Happy landings."

"Will you help me?"

"What for?"

"I could guarantee you certain rewards." She grinned impishly.

"Sex isn't a reward with me, baby. It's a functional necessity. Like lunch. Got any better offers?"

Lois snubbed out her cigarette in an ashtray, glanced at me and picked up her handbag. She smiled, cocked her head and said, "Give me time. I'll think of something."

I waited until she was almost out. "Lois . . ."

She looked back at me. "Yes?"

"What are you after?"

"Have you gone through your deceased friend's things yet?"

"Casually."

"Did he traffic in bananas?"

"Beats me."

She smiled again. "If you find out, I'm at the Jackson Hotel."

"Swell. I'll bring a bottle."

"Why waste time drinking?"

"Yeah," I said as she closed the door.

Bananas! Now it was bananas. What was it Tuck's letter said? . . . "Don't choke on a banana."

I got Charlie Traub, two of his assistants and three girls from the office. We spent the rest of the day going through every piece of paper in the files. There wasn't a thing mentioning bananas anywhere. I said the hell with it, went back to my motel unit to clean up for supper. The second I stepped inside the darkened room I knew I'd been had. The first solid *thwack* caught me rolling away but brought me to my knees. The second one did the job and was almost a relief. The sudden swell of unconsciousness blotted out the terribly explosive pain that seemed to be bottled up inside my skull, dulling it little by little until it was only a memory.

There were three of them there: two small dark men in grey business suits and a taller, sardonic type who sat comfortably in a chair, watching me with mild amusement.

I lay on the floor at his feet, my legs drawn up behind me and taped to my wrists behind my back. A piece of the same adhesive had been plastered across my mouth so that the low moan of pain I let out seemed to come through my nose. Each eye was a separate ball of torture, the ache in my head seeming to be concentrated at the pupils. Every pulse beat was an individual torture.

Either the pain moderated or my tolerance to it increased, because I could see and hear again. There was wind, but it came from outside the building, gusts rattling the palm leaves and whistling as they twisted past the corners of the motel.

"Feeling better, Mr. Fallon?" His eyes danced again and the pencil-line mustache twisted as he smiled.

All I could do was glare at him.

"Don't try to talk. Until you fully understand your predicament, I merely want you to listen and understand. Then you may speak. Let me remind you—one attempt to draw attention here and you will regret it." He turned his head to the man beside him. "Juan . . ."

With a practiced move, the little guy flipped open a knife.

"It can be painful, Mr. Fallon."

He didn't have to point it out. I'd seen it all done before. I let my eyes wander past his face and take in the room. They had destroyed it pretty well. The one in the chair smiled again. He reached inside his coat and found an envelope. When he pulled out the letter, I saw it was the note Tucker had left for me.

"I'm going to remove the tape from your mouth, Mr. Fallon. I want you to explain something, and if it is satisfactory we will simply leave you here. Frankly, dead men can cause trouble. However, you can make me kill you, if you wish. Your life is a very impersonal matter. Do you understand?"

I nodded. I had done business with these types before.

"Take off the tape."

The man with the knife bent over, felt for the edge of the adhesive like he was going to peel an apple, caught it and ripped it loose with a jerk. I felt the skin of my lips tear and I almost made a fatal mistake of trying to catch his nose with the top of my head. He grinned, realizing my intention, and squatted there with the knife, ready to slip it into my belly.

"You have control now?"

"I know the rules," I said.

"Good." He fingered the paper, holding it up so I could see it. "A carefully guarded note from your late friend, no?"

"No."

"Then why hide it where you did?"

174

"It wasn't hard to find. I just considered it personal, that's all."

"Perhaps. But I think you couldn't quite figure it out and kept it as a memorandum."

"Why?"

"Ah yes, why. We know that Tucker Stacy had little or no previous contact with you, so I agree that you have no knowledge or interest in his . . . let's say, ventures. However, as his inheritor, you do have now, and it is likely that you think to capitalize on *everything* he was involved in. Therefore you do not wish to let anything slip through your fingers. Reasonable?"

"Yeah, but not true," I grunted. "What the hell is this all about?"

"Who are Verdo and Cristy, Mr. Fallon?"

"I wish I knew."

"Ah, but you do."

"Sorry, buddy, but that's one thing you can't get from me. Whoever they are belongs to twenty years ago."

"Tucker Stacy seemed to think you would know them."

"He was wrong." It was the way I said it that made him frown.

"Yes, that could be, but there are ways of probing a man's mind to make him remember."

"So hypnotize me."

Very languidly, he screwed a cigarette into a holder. "You are in no position to be facetious, my friend."

"So go screw yourself then."

The little guy with the knife pricked the skin of my neck. He was enjoying his work.

I said, "What's this all about?"

"It is better that you don't know. None of it is your affair."

"Then you're at a dead end, buddy."

The tall one nodded and pulled at his cigarette, "If we could be sure of that, your chances of survival would be much improved."

There was a sudden shriek of metal and something smashed against the window frame. Like a cat, the little guy was at the light, snapped it off, then opened the door a crack to peer out. He turned, closed the door and flipped the light back on. "It is the window shutter, *Señor* Marcel. The wind . . ."

His voice cut off at the look the tall guy gave him. I faked a groan and laid my head back to cover the moment. *A name. At least I had a name now. Señor Marcel.*

When I opened my eyes he was watching me. Then, after a few seconds, he seemed to make his decision. I was a nothing. I couldn't have caught his name. "This note, Mr. Fallon . . . it mentions choking on a banana. Could you explain that?"

Inside my head the pounding started again. Cramp spasms were starting up my neck and all sensation was gone in my fingers. "I don't know what the hell he meant. Get off my back, will you?"

The knife touched me again. "Shall we try another way, *señor?*"

Marcel pulled the cigarette butt from the holder and dropped it into an ashtray. "No, not this time. I think our friend here is telling the truth. It is quite possible that he might learn something later. In that case we shall pay him another visit." He stepped toward me and looked down at me, his eyes cold little slips of ice. "You are a smart man, Mr. Fallon?"

I didn't answer him.

"If you are, you will say nothing about this. We have people around and if it is necessary to eliminate you I will be more than happy to accommodate. If you even become a nuisance, this will happen. You may, for instance, speculate on your friend Tucker Stacy."

Before I could grasp his meaning, he made a motion to the one with the knife, the tape was slapped on my mouth, and with a smile of pure pleasure he swung the sap at my head and the world was all dark, pinpricked with a million lights that went out one by one.

Chapter 5

I didn't realize I was awake until the beam of a light seared my eyes. I had been in a state of half consciousness when the flash beamed itself at my face, twisting a knife into my brain. A curiously lilting voice said, "Maybe this time I shall kill you, *señor*."

Sharon Ortiz.

It won't take much, I figured.

The light made a circuit of the moon, spotting the disorder and the strewn papers. "They found something," she accused. Then the light hit my face again. "You will tell me."

I was past the point of argument. I didn't care one way or another. There was a lot I wanted to tell her that could be summed up in two distinct words, but something always made me play the angles.

She leaned forward and caught the tape over my mouth by a corner. I squinted my eyes against what was to come, but unlike the others, she worked it loose carefully. "What was it?" she hissed.

"Bananas," I said. "That's all those damn fools wanted to know about."

Air whistled through her clenched teeth. "They know!"

"Nuts."

177

"Mr. Fallon!" I was looking right down the barrel of the .38 again.

I said, "He left me a note. He told me not to choke on a banana. Now drop dead. I'm sick and tired of being caught in the middle of all this."

Slowly, the gun dropped so that it pointed at the floor. The light bouncing off the tile threw a soft glow around her, making her hair shimmer like new coal. "Yes, I realize. You are typically American, *señor*. Nothing is of any importance to you except your dollar and yourself. You are making it so easy."

Sharon Ortiz knelt beside me and I felt her fingers at the tape behind my back. She stripped it off with a harsh, tearing sound, not trying to be gentle. Then she stood up to watch me writhe helplessly as the blood flowed back into my arms and legs.

"I don't think you are worth killing, *señor*. Maybe later, but not now."

"That's what everybody thinks."

"I hope your friend gave you good advice. Don't choke on a banana. If I were you I would not even look for one. Good night, *señor*."

For a half hour I lay there rubbing myself back to normal. When I could walk, I found a bottle of Four Roses in the kitchenette and mixed a drink. Damn Tuck and whatever he was up to. Why did he leave me trouble? I had enough on my own. Damn every one of them. I was tired of being kicked around like a stray dog. Well, the Capital K was mine now and I was going to run it. Nobody else. Just me and my way. You get one chance in life to cut out of the ditch and this was mine.

By mid-morning, Charlie Traub had the Mustang ready.

It was crouched in the hangar like the deadly, hungry thing it was, defanged now, but ready to scream back into the blue where it belonged. Charlie came over wiping his hands on a dirty rag, and when he looked at me his eyes narrowed.

He pointed out the hangar doors. "You going up? Wind's pretty stiff."

"Not enough to bother this bird."

"Ingrid is cutting in on Jamaica. Looks like she's coming this way. We ought to be tying down a lot of kites pretty soon."

"Good. Look, am I gassed up?"

"Ready to roll."

"Get her out on the ramp. I might want to take off in a hurry."

"Sure, Cat. Thought you wanted that jump seat installed, though."

"I'll tell you when. You see Trusky and Reed around?"

"Sure. Since six A.M. they've been asking everybody questions. What do you think they'll come up with?"

"What do *you* think, Charlie. You were closer to him than anyone else." I paused and studied him. "Was he involved with the Cubans?"

For ten seconds he stared out the door, then came back to me. "Sure he was, Cat. He was the contact man between Miami and the ones in Cuba trying to oust the Commies."

"How do you know, Charlie?"

"Like a maid who washes your clothes. She knows if you're clean or dirty. Some things you can't hide. Bullet holes in wing fabric, for instance. Sand in the fairings from beach landings. Certain fuel loadings and special harness rigs for cute drops and pickups. He had some good cover for what he was doing, but he didn't fool me none." He looked down at his hands and stuffed the rag in his back pocket.

"And whose side were you on, Charlie?"

His eyes bored into mine. "I hate that Commie bunch," he said.

I held out my hand. "I'm with you."

George Clinton was having lunch when I found him. He waved me over, put down his paper and offered me a cigar. He said, "I had a call from Slim Upgate to make sure you got what you needed. You got some big friends, buddy."

"I did him a favor once."

"Pays off. What can I do for you?"

"Any connections in Miami?"

"What kind?"

"Guns and ammo to the bunch in the mountains."

"You can check that through surplus sales."

"Not this time. The stuff would go through too many hands. Besides, a lot of arms dealers have held the stuff for years, waiting for something like this. It'll be strictly black market for these shipments. Our State Department isn't clearing anything through to Cuba the easy way."

"I know. They do everything bas-ackwards. Now they got real trouble on their hands."

"How about it?"

"Where can I reach you?"

"Suppose I call you. How long will it take?"

"Couple of hours."

"Where can I reach you?"

He jotted down a number on the back of a matchbook and handed it to me. "Keep your fingers crossed."

"Sure," I said. "And find out if anyone knows a guy named Marcel."

Clinton took the cigar out of his mouth slowly. "André Marcel?"

"Could be. Tall, thin guy with a mustache and an accent."

"You're asking for trouble, Fallon."

"That's all I been getting. Who is he?"

"If he were in the rackets, you'd call him an enforcer. He's a troubleshooter for any country with money to spend. The last I heard of Marcel he was operating in Panama. He was responsible for re-routing the drug traffic that used to come into the States from Algiers up through Italy and Spain. He saw to it that only the stuff out of China got in."

"So two birds got killed with one stone," I said.

"Right. The Red organization piled up loot and the moral breakdown was speeded up here with the influx of H."

I got up to leave.

"Fallon . . . How far is this going? Are we covered?"

"Nothing will involve you."

"Good. Let me know if you need a couple of hands. I know some boys who will be glad to do a favor for Slim, too."

I called Lois Hays from the lobby of the Jackson Hotel and was invited right up. When I knocked, she opened the door and stood there smiling at some secret joke, waiting while I took my time to look at her.

The sheer black negligee was all she had on, carefully arranged so that the neckline plunged in a wide open V that laid bare half her breasts before it swept into a knotted belt.

"Like?" she asked.

"Neat, but not gaudy," I said.

She chuckled and led me into the room, quite conscious of the fact that the sun streaming through the window in the far wall did more than just silhouette her figure. It illuminated it with cleverly distorted shadows that were uncomfortable to watch. Sitting down was another contrived production designed to jolt the stability of any situation. Almost carelessly, she crossed her legs and let the flesh of her thighs sparkle through the slit in the gown.

181

I showed my appreciation and looked—like I was supposed to. The only trouble was that there was nothing new about it. But women never seem to take that into consideration.

"You said you'd bring a bottle."

"And you said why waste time."

"So?"

"You were right. There's more to do."

"And what's that supposed to mean?"

"Bananas. You asked me about them. So has everybody else."

I slid into a chair beside the phone and glanced at my watch. "You brought the bit up, so you must know something about it. You're in the news business. You're covering something to do with the Cuban situation. Whatever the bananas are, they're not quite a secret and since I'm involved I'd like to be let in a little bit more before I stick my neck out."

"And how far will that be, Mr. Fallon?"

I watched her a few moments, then I said, "All the way, kid. Somehow it revolves around me. I don't know how, but I intend to find out. I got the strange idea that without me the whole thing can't work."

"Possibly," she told me.

"Or something else."

She paused in the act of reaching for a cigarette. "And what might that be?"

"Maybe it's just necessary to be sure I *don't* know anything—because if I did I might want to follow through on what Tuck started."

"What do you intend doing?"

"I'm going to satisfy my curiosity, sugar."

"That's what killed the cat."

"Not this cat. Can I use the phone?" She waved her hand

182

to go ahead. "Long distance?" I asked.

"It'll go on expenses." She snubbed the cigarette out and unfolded from the chair. "I'll get dressed."

The long-distance operator made a good missing persons tracer. She started with an obsolete number, but finally ran down Joe Conway operating a propeller rebuilding shop in south Jersey. He was another guy from the old 252nd Fighter Squadron whom I had seen on rare occasions since the war. He had put in a lot of pub time in London with us. Like Tuck, Joe had known practically everybody on the base.

For ten minutes, he rehashed the old days in a bubble of enthusiasm before he realized there was something I wanted. He had read of Tuck's death and didn't seem surprised at me inheriting his estate. All I told him was that Tuck mentioned two other guys and wanted me to look them up—Verdo and Christy.

After a moment's silence, Joe said, "Jeez, pal, those names are familiar, but I'll be damned if I remember who they are. You sure they were with our outfit?"

"They must have been. Think they were late replacements?"

"Could be, but I knew most of those, too. This real important?"

"Yeah."

"Tell you what. I see Whitey Thompson once in a while, and he has an album full of pictures of the old bunch. Suppose I go over what he has and see what I can do."

"I'd appreciate it, Joe."

"I'll get right on it. Keep your head out of the cockpit."

"You know me."

When I hung up, I dialed George Clinton to see if he had found anything out. "Cat Fallon, George. Find your man?"

There was a small hesitation, then, "Yeah, I got him."

"Well?"

"Your buddy Tucker Stacy was working against the Castro bunch, all right. He was making arms drops, but from what I gather it was more of a cover for something else. He was closer to the political situation."

"What do you mean?"

"He was hauling important people in and out of Cuba, working on the big end. Now listen, these people of mine have funny sources of information. It's damn reliable, and in their kind of work they have to be sure of the score. At the same time, they don't want to get involved. They come up with more stuff than the CIA. You know what happens if any of this leaks through you? Even Slim Upgate won't try to help you."

"I'm clued in, buddy."

"Okay then. Ever since the Bay of Pigs, something big has been in the works down in Cuba. Nobody seems to know what it really is, but it's mighty explosive. Our own agencies have been working on it and running up against a wall. Whenever someone gets inside the Castro outfit and learns something, they never show up again, so their counterespionage must be pretty good. Whatever's going on, Stacy was wise to it. He got so hot none of the boys would do business with him. They'll peddle guns, ammo, equipment—but nix on politics. They can be hit from both ends if they try."

"How about André Marcel?"

"A Castro boy. He doesn't give a damn about arms shipments because the Reds can out-supply anything the black market can send over from the U.S. He's strictly political. A rough guy. I'll tell you something else, too. Nobody seems to think Stacy died accidentally. He had some live cargo with him when he went down, somebody from the hills with proof of what was going on down there."

I said, "That's all?"

"That's all anybody will talk about. What comes next?"

"A trip to Miami. I want to find out a little more about that accident. And give me a contact there."

"Try Felix Ramsey at the Cable-Hurley Supplies Company. It's listed in the book. Felix runs the operation from behind the scenes. He'll go along with whatever you want as long as it's in line with policy."

"Got it. Thanks."

"Good luck. You want my boys?"

"I'll handle it."

When he hung up, I called Upgate in New York and passed on the word. Slim seemed pleased and wished me luck, too, without asking what I was doing. I cradled the phone and sat there thinking the thing through. But it still boiled down to just one thing . . . who were Cristy and Verdo?

"Do I look all right?" she said from the doorway.

Lois Hayes was sheathed in black, the sheen of a soft fabric clinging to the curves of her body. A wide belt nipped her in at the waist, giving the thrust of her breasts the look of aggressive jetpods on a Boeing 707. I had to laugh.

She frowned. "What's so funny?"

"Nothing. What's the outfit for?"

"I thought you'd take me with you."

"Why?"

"Because you're looking for something. So am I. It may be the same thing."

"What'll you do with it when you find it, kid?"

She took a few long-legged strides into the room so I could get the full effect. "I want to write about it. That's my job."

For an instant she had that dedicated look again, then she turned slowly and gave me the total charge of those deep blue eyes. "Will you take me?"

I shrugged. "Why not. Maybe you can pull some strings I can't. Only let's go now before I get sexy."

Chapter 6

Hurricane Ingrid had picked up speed since the last weather check. Miami had it at full strength with winds over the 100 mph mark and alerts going out all along the coast. So far the state was only tasting the far-reaching effects of scud and heavy gusts, but in a few more days Ingrid was going to tear things apart if she stayed on course. The patrol planes had it heading directly for Cuba, and if it followed the normal track, it would continue toward Florida.

Charlie Traub felt a little uneasy about me going out, but I filed a flight plan for Miami, made a visual check of the Mustang and helped Lois into the jump seat. She wasn't going to be comfortable and I didn't care, but there was no word of complaint from her at all. Installing that back seat knocked out the fuselage tank, but I didn't need the range much.

I started up, checked the mags at the end of the runway and got a tower clearance for take-off. Once in the air, I switched to the Miami frequency and stayed on a heading until the airfield was in sight.

Lois made my first contact for me, a local reporter named DeWitt who had written the original story of Tuck's disappearance—the one the wire services picked up. We met over coffee in a restaurant and he laid out a folder of clips on the incident. There were several pictures of Tuck beside a plane at the Capital K, one at a ground-breaking ceremony somewhere in Celada and another taken outside the state capitol.

Most of the copy was devoted to his activities in helping build Celada from a nothing town to a national tourist spot, but because of the unknown factors surrounding his death, the details mainly centered on the squall line he was supposedly caught up in, the extent of the search and the statement of the helicopter pilots who spotted the wreckage and the fisherman who collected a few fragments.

I jotted down the names of the pilots and the fisherman, thanked DeWitt and got on the phone to the airbase. Captain Rob Olsen was on alert but at his home, and when I located him he said he'd meet me at the club in an hour. This time I let Lois rent a U-Drive-It on her credit card and drove on out to the field.

The captain's story was concise . . . it was a routine search mission in a given area that extended no more than ten miles off shore on the supposition that Tuck had simply tried to skirt the storm and got caught up in it. He had pictures of the pieces of flotsam from the Staggerwing Beech. Enlarged, they showed a seat cushion, pieces of fabrics and a dented GI gas can with a familiar white hand and a large K beneath it. Twisted around the can were unmistakable parts of aircraft framing and more fabric. Since his helicopter was not equipped with floats, Captain Olsen had not made an attempt at pickup, but radioed the location to his base. Then a boat was sent out. However, before the patrol boat arrived, the fisherman got there, attracted by the chopper, salvaged the wreckage and later handed the remains over to the government launch.

Before we left, I told Captain Olsen I was a pilot, briefed him on my background and asked him what he thought of the squall line.

"That's the funny part," he told me. "It wasn't that bad. The Beech could have made it without any trouble, I'd say, but you know thunderheads. Maybe he hit it at the wrong spot."

"But it *could* have been torn up in the storm?"

"It could have been."

"Thanks, Captain."

Later Lois said, "What now?"

"I want to be certain of something."

"Do you mind telling me what you are really after?"

"I don't think you'd understand."

"Why not?"

"Because you aren't curious enough, honey. You sit and listen while I talk—like you knew all along what's going on and are just letting things stall out. You're supposed to be a reporter with a newsy nose. You gather facts for a political hack who is always after our government policy, but you aren't prying a bit."

She made a wry face. "All right, I know what you're after."

"Tell me."

"You want to know how Tucker Stacy died."

I grinned at her. "I know that, sugar. I want to know why."

"Go right ahead then. You're doing fine. You'll make a good story yourself if nothing comes of this one. It you have something more specific for me to do . . ."

"I have."

"What?"

"Miami is loaded with anti-Castro people. You know any of them?"

"There are some who have appealed to our government. There's their government-in-exile and . . ."

"Okay, try them. Get to the big ones and see what you can come up with on this bananas thing."

Her eyes darted to my face.

"You got it from someplace. Where?"

She licked her lips, then: "A rumor. The person who mentioned it was killed before he could testify before a Congressional committee."

"That Gonzales guy last week?" I asked.

"Uh-huh. He had come over in a small boat that had floundered halfway across and drifted for a week. He was near dead from exhaustion and exposure. I was there when they took him off the rescue boat. I heard him mention the word."

"So he was hungry."

"Could be."

"Suppose you find out. Think you know the right people?"

Lois nodded. "I can try. Shall we meet later?"

"There's a Paramount Motel across from where we rented the car. I'll stay there tonight."

She started to smile.

"Two rooms," I said.

The smile turned into a pout.

"Adjoining," I added.

"I'd like that," she said.

Rather than have DeWitt come out again, I went to the office and had him show me the editions of the paper that carried the account of Gonzales' death. When he didn't appear for the hearing, he was found choked to death in his roominghouse near Washington—even though a police officer guarded the building. Investigation showed that the killer had gained entry by climbing a tree in the backyard, forcing a second-floor window and making his exit the same way. It was assumed the killer was a Castro fanatic.

DeWitt said, "That wasn't the first one of those."

"Oh?"

"This town is loaded with people from both sides. Hell,

it's open warfare around here no matter whom you favor. Luckily for us, they keep it pretty much inside their own quarter, but the situation is going to blow someday. By the way, you know who this guy Gonzales was?"

"Nope."

He thumbed through some later editions and pulled one out on its rack. The story was on page four, a resume of the rescue and subsequent murder of Gonzales. It said he was formerly employed by one of the ousted American industries in Havana.

After I finished, I said, "What about it?"

"Nothing much," he shrugged. "Up until now they'd been playing the guy like he was a peasant climbing off the farm. Turns out he was a chemical engineer. What I'd like to know is what he wanted to spill to the Congressional committee."

"I don't think it would matter. They never seem to listen to anybody anyway."

"That's how it goes. Need anything else?"

"Where can I find that fisherman?"

"The one who picked up the plane wreckage?"

"Uh-huh."

He told me to wait, dug into some other files until he found what he wanted and handed me a slip of paper with a name and address on it.

Peter Claude Watworthy was a dried-up little guy who had spent too many years in the sun. His face, neck and hands were withered and brown, but toughened to a leathery consistency. He sat on the back of his trailer puffing a pipe, staring into the sunset with obvious pleasures and let me speak my piece.

Finally, he put the pipe down and propped his feet up on a crate. "I been wondering about that, too, son. Up to now, nobody's asked me—and I ain't about to be traipsing off tellin' what's none of my business anyway."

"Mind talking about it?"

He knocked the ashes out of his pipe and started stumping in a fresh load. "Not at all, son. Like to talk, matter of fact. Don't get much chance to any more, seems like. You want to know about that airplane, huh?"

"Anything you can tell me."

"Well, I think the papers got it all wrong."

"How's that, Mr. Watworthy."

"Peter Claude's the name."

"Sure."

"I been out three days fishing when it happened. Now I ain't saying I'm sure, y'hear? I'm saying what I *think*."

"That's good enough."

"The night of that storm . . . after it was all over . . . I seen this flash in the sky. Could've been a rocket a long way off, could've been anything else. Anyway, there was just that one flash. Around here, you get so you take things into consideration. Nothin' I could do about it, and since nothin' came over the radio I just forgot about it. It wasn't until two days later I saw that there helicopter and went looking to see what the trouble was. That was when I found the stuff in the water and gave it to the government men when they come out.

"Peculiar thing was, if that plane went down in the storm, the stuff would've wound up on the shore by then. If it did come from the flash I seen, it was about in the right place."

Impatiently, I sat and made nothing out of it.

"Later, I got to thinking about something else I found," the old man went on. He eased off the seat and shuffled toward the cabin where he rummaged around in a box. When he came back he had the handle and part of a suitcase in his fingers.

I took it from him, examined the charred edges and the peculiar way the leather was shredded into its fibrous parts. One end of the handle broke loose and I saw where the brass clasp had been almost melted.

"Got that out a way, near where the flash was." He paused. "Ever see anything like that before?" he asked.

I nodded. "I've seen bomb damage do things like this to leather."

"Dynamite, son. I seen it happen, too. Now you know what I've been thinking?"

"I think you're right, Peter Claude." I handed the fragment back to him. "Hold on to this in case I need it."

"Trouble, son?"

"There's always trouble, Peter Claude."

"How right you are, son."

When I reached the Paramount Motel, I picked a Coke out of the machine and stuck my key in the lock. I closed the door, flipped the light on and the Coke stopped halfway to my mouth. "What the hell . . ."

"Come right in, Mr. Fallon," Del Reed said. He pointed to the two sitting on opposite sides of the room, big men with bland faces that had the mark of government service stamped on them.

"Do you have a warrant, Reed?"

"Do we need one?"

"Okay, what do you want?" I glanced around the place. "How'd you find me here?"

"We've had a tail on you, friend. I'm glad you were truthful about your flight plan. We picked you up the minute you got here. You've been asking a lot of questions."

"Your business?"

"We're making it that. These gentlemen are federal

agents. Mr. Smith and Mr. Jones. Improbable names, but theirs nevertheless."

"So what?"

"If you care to be inconvenienced, it can be done. It's your choice now."

"I don't get it," I said.

Jones, the heavy one, spoke, scarcely moving his month. "We've run a pretty thorough check on you, Fallon. You have a few things in your immediate past that might not stand a good investigation."

I put the Coke down and sat on the arm of a chair. "Kill it, buddies, I've had the con by the experts. This you'd do sure enough, except for one thing."

"And what would that be?" Jones asked.

"Time. You need time. You want to know something. Okay, so do I, so quit wasting time."

They passed a quick look between them and the other one nodded. Jones said, "Sometimes we have to take certain risks in this business. But first let me tell you something . . . from this moment on, you'll be involved with national security. Break it and you've had it. Clear enough?"

"Clear enough," I repeated.

"You know what you're doing?" Del said angrily.

"Keep quiet, Reed," Jones told him. "It's out of your hands now." He leaned forward, staring at me. "When the Russians folded in Cuba, they shipped their missiles out. Aerial photos showed them lashed to the decks of ships, and information from our agents confirmed the fact up to a certain extent."

"Go on."

"Whether or not the nuclear warheads were removed couldn't be proved. Let's suppose something, Mr. Fallon. Suppose one of those devices were installed in a ship and that ship headed for some strategic port here in the States and blown while it was docked."

He stopped there and sat back, waiting for me to digest it.

Finally, I said, "So that's what 'banana' is."

The look went between them again. "What's that, Mr. Fallon?"

"Banana. It's a boat. A ship."

"Where did you find that out?"

"Tucker Stacy mentioned it in passing."

"No jokes, Fallon."

"Is it a ship?" I asked softly.

"Yes. That isn't the name, but it's a ship. It's a code name the Cuban underground gave it."

I looked at the three of them. "Where is it?"

"Someplace at sea."

"You don't know?"

"We can't get inside the hurricane area to find out. It cleared Cuba to get away from the storm and that's all we know. But what we want is . . . what do *you* know, Mr. Fallon?"

"No more than you do, but Tuck knew about it."

"We knew he was involved with them. What else did he tell you?"

"Nothing, but it was obvious why he was killed."

Jones's eyes narrowed at the word. "That's right, he was murdered. Apparently he was bringing someone back from Cuba in the Beech and a dynamite bomb got loaded aboard with him. Somebody else had to get out fast with the information so Gonzales went. He got knocked off before he could talk too."

Jones grunted, "Stupid."

"Why?"

"We should have had him before the committee. They

194

wanted him recovered from the trip. We could have gotten the information earlier. Damn amateurs." He took a heavy breath and settled back. "That isn't locating the ship, Fallon."

"You won't get it from me. That's all I know."

This time it was Smith who spoke. His voice was a hoarse growl that didn't go with his face. "We're beginning to wonder. You might have a personal angle."

"Like what?"

"The Hays woman. It could be a pay-off for a news story. It could be something else."

I just looked at him.

"You're looking for a kick in the teeth, boy."

"It's just a thought we'll keep in mind. I hope you don't plan on going anywhere soon."

"Why?"

"Because I'm going to be your closest companion until this thing gets settled. Someplace in your mind you got a bug. It says you got something we want to know. I've been in this business too long not to smell things like that—and sooner or later I'm going to get it out of you."

"Lots of luck."

He ignored the crack. "Tucker Stacy told you something else. You're still thinking about it. I want to be around when you find out what it is."

Jones and Del Reed got up then, but Smith didn't move. They weren't kidding anymore. They said good night pleasantly, opened the door and left. I looked at Smith and he grinned, then switched on the TV. A newscaster appeared. Hurricane Ingrid was a blaster. All ships were being warned out of the area and the local citizens were being warned to batten down. Ingrid was over Cuba, still on course, picking up speed and increasing in wind velocity.

I walked to the phone, told the switchboard operator to get me a direct line and take time and charges, then I dialed through to George Conway up in Jersey. I asked him if he had seen Whitey Thompson about his old squadron pictures.

"Got right to him, Cat. Look, we went over everything, but he couldn't remember anybody named Cristy and Verdo. He wanted to know, could it've been a squadron call name or anythin'? He remembers the names, but not who they belonged to."

"We were all color and animal calls, George. Red three and four, Tiger Two . . . you know."

"I'll keep working on it. You'll call me back?"

"Roger."

I hung up and went back to watching television. Verdo and Cristy! Who were they? What were they? They hung there in the past of 20 years ago, meaning something Tucker thought I'd understand without any trouble at all. Why? What made him think I'd get the angle? So we were fighter pilots. We flew Mustangs and escorted B-17s and B-24s in and out of Germany. We did some low-level strafing, a little photo-recon work, covered the invasion and horsed around London. What else? I couldn't figure it. I squatted down on the edge of the bed and gave up.

Lois Hays was due in. It was going to be a long night.

Maybe. The little gust of air on my neck turned me around.

Smith turned, too, and died before he ever saw who it was. The bullet from the silenced gun caught him right in the middle of his forehead.

André Marcel said, "You have been speaking to the wrong people, my friend. Now you will come with us. You will speak with us, too, and if you will speak well you will die quickly like your government friend there—not slowly like so many others have died before him."

Chapter 7

It was a small room filled with the smell of the sea, and I could hear the waves lashing at pilings beneath my feet. The wind was alternately shrill and sorrowful, building in strength.

They had me on a table, stripped to the skin, an overhead light blazing in my eyes. The hypo had worn off and I was fully awake. I could feel my heart pounding inside my chest. André stood above me, the two goons on either side. Very delicately he ran a finger over two scars on my body. "I've seen these marks before, Mr. Fallon. They were professionally inflicted."

"Algiers," I said. "I'm still here."

"Quite. They never had a chance to finish, did they?"

A shudder ran through me, I wasn't as brave as I thought. I strained at the ropes that held me spread-eagled. I was lucky the last time in Algiers. The French had come just in time. And I couldn't have talked because I had nothing to say. Still, the Wogs would have gone ahead with the job. It was that way now, too.

"You are familiar with Arab torture?"

I didn't answer him.

"Ah, I see you are. In that case, let us forego a few of the more basic steps and come quickly to those appliances that seem to guarantee results." He reached for something attached to the table and brought up a pair of insulated wires. On the end of each one was a battery clip that could carry a lot of amperage.

"In case you have forgotten, this is an unusual instrument.

One end we attach like so . . ." André Marcel snagged the clip in my earlobe. I winced, but it was nothing compared to what was to come.

"The other end," he said, "will be attached to your testicles. At given intervals, a switch will be thrown and . . . ah, I see you realize what will happen. Not only is it most painful, but totally destructive. You would no longer be a man *if* you lived. You would never again know a woman or even want to. Most probably, however, you would die right here after hours of living with the pain centered in your vitals. Unpleasant to contemplate, isn't it, Fallon."

"You haven't got long to live, Marcel."

"So! You did catch my name." He looked at the guy beside him. "You see?"

The one he addressed twitched nervously. Mistakes could be fatal in his business.

"Still," André said with a humorless smile, "like you, I am still alive, but my chances of survival are better. Now, shall we proceed?"

"I can't tell you what I don't know."

"We shall see. First, what did you tell the government police?"

Sweat ran into my eyes and started to burn. I played it cagey and gave him facts. He would know them anyway. "They know Stacy was killed because he was trying to get information back about the nuclear warhead on the ship."

"What ship?"

"You call it *Banana*."

Marcel nodded slowly. "Good. You are telling the truth. Where is that ship going?"

"I don't know."

He reached out and jammed the clip up between my legs and the teeth bit into me. I started to yell when he said, "The

198

switch, please," and the yell rose into a wild scream that didn't sound like my own voice at all. When it stopped, the sweat poured down my face and my whole body jerked spasmodically for a moment before the pain came.

Marcel let me taste it fully, let me realize that it was only that of a second's duration, let me imagine what it would be like if it had continued longer. "Who are Verdo and Cristy, Mr. Fallon?"

I shook my head. I saw his nod toward the one at the switch and I tried to tell him that I didn't know anything—but my tongue seemed to bloat suddenly at the incredible sweep of pain that came over me like a tidal wave of liquid fire.

When I tried to talk, my lips couldn't form the words and my chest heaved convulsively. The sticky warmth of blood trickled down my wrists and ankles from where the ropes bit in when I strained against them. The sheer terror of knowing that there was nothing I could say turned my brain into a mad thing.

"You will have a minute to speculate, Fallon. Time to recover, time to reconsider, then we will begin again."

My mind raced with something to tell him. *Verdo and Cristy, Verdo and Cristy. They alone could break me loose from this. Who the hell were they? Who? WHO!*

"Very well, Fallon, once again, who are Verdo and Cristy?"

He was ready to nod again. Then I had it. I had Verdo and Cristy. Not who, *what!*

And I was going to tell him. The hell with them all. He could have it.

The blast from Sharon Ortiz' gun caught the guy at the switch full in the face. His head came apart in pieces, and before they could hit the floor she nailed the other one in the chest. He fell into André Marcel enough to ruin his aim and tumble him to the floor on one knee. I could see his expression as he looked up at her, the almost simpering grin of an idiot not knowing what to do yet knowing too what was coming. He started to make an imploring gesture when Sharon smiled back at him and almost casually pulled the trigger of the .38.

The first bullet hit Marcel in the stomach and he grabbed his gut as he doubled over. He looked up imploringly, holding his hand out, and the next one went through his palm into his chest. It slammed him back into the table where he coughed once and said something foul in Spanish. Then Sharon took deliberate aim and planted one right between the horns.

Very gently, she removed the clips attached to me. Then wiped the sweat from my face with her scarf. "You have not been hurt, *señor*. They had a long way to go before you were hurt."

"Get me loose," I breathed.

"First I must look at you."

"Damn you."

"Why, *señor?* I remember you looking at me like so not long ago. Can you imagine the things I could do to you now?"

I didn't answer her.

Then she smiled. "But they would not be unpleasant," she said.

In spite of what had just happened, I felt some crazy things go through my mind. "Stop it."

Deliberately, she did something, then grinned again and reached in the pocket of her coat and pulled out a small knife. It took only a second to cut me loose. My clothes were in the corner on a chair and I dressed while she watched, never without that damn smile. She didn't know it yet, but for this she was going to get fixed. Soon and good.

I said, "How long were you outside?"

"Long enough to know you wouldn't tell them anything, *señor*."

She didn't know, I thought. *She was wrong, but she didn't know.*

Sharon changed then. The smile faded and a look of serious concern crossed her eyes. "I know whose side you are on now, *señor*."

The shadows dancing across her face gave a different life to her beauty. Her hair was a deep midnight glow, her lips lushly ruby, the Irish and Spanish in her trying to come out at the same time. I felt the firm swell of her breasts brush against my forearm and I ran my hand up her shoulder. Beneath her suit coat, she was warm and a muscle under my fingers trembled.

"How did you find me, Sharon?"

"By following André Marcel. He is so smart as to be stupid sometimes. He does not realize that our organization is also efficient. We are small, perhaps, but necessarily efficient. I knew he would keep contact with you. You are the key, *señor*, to all that we have."

"I know what the score is now, honey," I said. "The whole deal. I know about the ship you called *Banana*."

"And where it is going?"

"Not yet."

Stark disappointment flooded her face.

"In a little while, kid, just a few minutes more. Look, where are we?"

"On a wharf in the south end."

"There's a phone nearby?"

"I know where one is."

"Good, let's find it."

I got Charlie Traub out of bed and asked him if Tucker

201

had ever taped any of his plane-to-tower conversations.

He said, "Sure, whenever he wanted a permanent record the tower operators would cut in a tape. Why?"

"Back in the old days, Verdo and Cristy were wire recording devices we could call while in flight on photo-recon missions if we spotted something in a hurry and didn't have time to jot it down. It was a squadron deal our own intelligence officer installed. Tuck still used the system, but with tape. You have a recorder handy?"

"One in the tower."

"Okay, put me on that extension and get up there. Get out the tapes of Tuck's last day. He may have called in, and if it was an automatic setup the tower operator never knew what was on there and just filed the thing."

When he made the exchange of extensions, I held on and got the rest of the information from Sharon. They had definite information on the removal of the warheads and the installation in the ship, but Castro's security was so tight that's all they had. A top agent named Manuel Alvada was to come out with Tucker with documented evidence of the switch, but the plane had been sabotaged by André Marcel's men. Gonzales was a technician who had stayed on in Cuba deliberately with intent to buck Castro and the know-how to get inside their major operations. When he defected they knew why and waited for him to show up in the States, Marcel preceding him there. The one thing he didn't know, however, was where the ship was headed.

Charlie came on then.

"Ready on the tapes."

"Roll it."

I heard Tuck's voice then, the drone of the engine in the background. Very calmly he stated his position and the fact that he was flying out an anti-Castro agent with the story of

Banana. He was taking no chances. In the event something happened before he could land he wanted the statement on record even if it wasn't documented.

Banana was a World War II Liberty ship named *Leona*. It was scheduled to sail for the Panama Canal where it would be blown up. It was to be quite a coup. In this day of the airlift and almost overnight reconstruction, the damage wouldn't be enough to impair our military or economic might. But that wasn't the intent of *Banana*. It was a propaganda program the Reds had set up that would work against us. With all the unrest in Central America, the *Leona* would blow and the Commies would say that it was a deliberate United States action to give us a chance to move directly into South American countries to "protect" them—thus offsetting a true people's movement against capitalistic governments. To back them up would be proof that the Panama Canal was an almost outdated project in these modern days of transportation, not even large enough to take modern carriers or battlewagons.

The cold war would become hot. The Reds had a live excuse of their own to move in militarily and the shooting would start. With the Red propaganda machine rolling, who would be on our side? Great!

Tuck's voice suddenly cut off. He had died.

I hung up and explained it to Sharon. I watched her pale. "It's too late, isn't it, *señor?*"

"Not now, not after all that's happened," I said. "It's never too late, Sharon." I looked up the number George Clinton gave me. I got the watchman at Cable-Hurley Supplies Company and he gave me Felix Ramsey's home number.

Ramsey didn't like me dragging him out of the sack, but when I mentioned Slim Upgate he was ready to do anything. I nailed it fast. I wanted two 500-pound demolition bombs to swing under the Mustang and I wanted them installed right away. He stuttered a little when I told him, but he said he'd have a truck out at the field in an hour.

I had one more call to make. This one was the big one. I got the man named Jones after three tries and told him to listen carefully and not bother tracing the call. I told him Smith was dead and so was the guy who killed him. I told him where they were. I also told him there was only one way the thing could be handled, and it was my way. If our government stepped in there would be hell to pay and the propaganda bit would go right on, but modified a little. The Reds would play up the attempt but capitalize on the fact that when they blew the whistle on the plot it was their men who were killed performing a public service and the U.S. who tried to destroy the evidence of it. It was all very neat and covered from every angle.

Calmly, Jones said, "Then how will it be done?"

"I'll do it. They'll never come back to me, brother."

"And you want what from me?"

"Get the reports from the planes patrolling the hurricane area. One of them might have spotted that ship. Can do?"

"Will do. How do I reach you?"

"I'll call you from another phone," I said and hung up.

The men were waiting by the Mustang with a truck. It didn't take long to swing the two bombs under the wing or to hook them up. When they were ready, the guys simply looked at me curiously and drove away.

I made the call to Jones. He had the information at hand, but his voice sounded shaky. He started, "Listen, Fallon . . ."

"No time, friend, this is it. When it's over I'll explain. Not now. What about that ship?"

"She was spotted. In fact, the planes directed her through the best section of the blow." He gave me the last coordinates and I wrote them down. "I know what you're planning, baby. You got me on a hook and I can't say a thing."

"Don't try."

She was waiting for me by the plane, her eyes shiny with tears. "You think you can do this thing?"

"I'm going to try like hell, baby."

"Then take my love with you, *señor*." She reached up, her arms going around my neck and her mouth was a volcanic thing of sweetness and fire that said everything at once, promising everything, and I remembered what she did to save my life and felt a wild hunger for the woman she was, full and glossy, vibrant with a love she was giving to me.

When I took my mouth away from hers I said, "I'll be back, Sharon," then I climbed in the old 11-51 and went through the starting procedure.

The tower didn't want to clear me, but I never gave him a chance to tell me so. I headed into the wind and eased the throttle forward and fought the side gusts until I was off the ground. Then I climbed to 30,000 feet, over the storm picked up my heading, held everything at max cruise and waited. The moon above made the rolling clouds of Ingrid look like grey snowbanks that gave way to the 60-mile width of the hurricane's eye before narrowing across its southeast quarter. Then I passed it.

Chapter 8

I found the *Leona* ten miles off her course estimate. To make sure, I swept in low with my landing lights on, wheels and flaps down. There was her name plastered across the stern in fading white paint. I got the gear retracted before the first bursts of gunfire winked at me from the decks. I picked up altitude and circled the ship below.

Two chances, that was all I had.

I made the first pass from the stern, dumping her over from 15,000 feet and releasing my bomb at 2000. Behind me came a shuddering *whump,* and when I looked back I could see the yellow glow of the burst and the lurch of the ship as she caught the near miss. There were lights on the deck now and in their beams I could see the ant-like figures of men running. A spot flicked on and tried to catch me, but there wasn't much chance of that. If they knew what they were carrying they'd be worrying about saving themselves, not killing me.

I took the Mustang up again and got set for another pass. I started to make a 180-degree turn into the run when I felt a sudden lightening of the ship, a quick uplift on the left wing and the insides wanted to drain out of me. Down below, the other bomb tore harmlessly into open water a half mile from the *Leona.*

It was too late after all.

For one second I thought of a suicide run, but I didn't have the guts for it. In helpless anger I circled over the *Leona,* cursing that battered old hulk and wishing I still had the six .50s mounted that could at least tear some holes in her, damning the idiots that mounted the bomb, but mainly damning myself for not having checked everything out.

I took one last look below. This time there *was* something different. The ship had stopped. It had heeled over sharply to port and was low in the water. I took another chance and went in again with the gear down and the lights on. I saw what had happened.

The first bird had been a near miss, all right, but those rusted plates of the ship's bottom were too old to take the concussion. They had folded and I had won. Damn it, *we* had won!

206

I eased the stick over and got out of there, getting on a return heading. But I couldn't help looking back. I was far and high enough away to see it safely when it went off. No big flash. No mushroom cloud. The *Leona* must have been underwater when it happened. Just a beautiful, diffused glow that changed colors in a soft pattern that rippled out gently and just as gently receded.

Ingrid came into sight again, her eye and front quarter reaching out for Florida. I beat her in and taxied up to the hangar where Sharon was still waiting, the wind whipping the dress tight around her legs. The tower was trying hard to get me to get under cover and the lights of a truck were coming toward me. I waved the truck off, motioned that I was going up again and the guy yelled something unintelligible and swung around.

As he did, the motor coughed twice and began to run rough until I idled it at higher RPM's. The old trouble was back again, despite Charlie's work. I wouldn't be able to shut down and re-start now without getting into it—and I wanted to get the hell out of there.

I edged in close to the hangar doors where there was a windbreak, locked the breaks, hopped out and chocked the wheels.

It was a bad thing to do, but I had no alternative.

Sharon came into my arms with a rush, burying her face in my chest, sobs of joy coming from her like that of a happy puppy. I shouted over the roar of the engine behind me, "She's gone. It's all right now . . . we have it made."

"As long as I have you back, my big one . . ."

"Inside. I have one call to make."

I pushed her ahead of me through the door into the hangar and felt for the light. The place was empty; everybody had cleared out in advance of Ingrid. I picked the phone off the wall and dialed my number.

The voice in the doorway said, "Hang up, Fallon."

We both turned around.

Lois Hays stood there, her face a mask of pure hatred, the gun in her hand a cold, deadly thing. I put the phone back.

"Yes, I'm sure of it now, Lois, I knew how Del Reed, Jones and Smith could have found me, but not André Marcel. You were the only one who knew about the Paramount Motel."

"You're quite right. I told him."

Outside, the wind was a tearing shriek. Ingrid was here. So was death. I felt Sharon's hand grope for mine, find it and hold tight.

I said, "It's too late, Lois. The *Leona* is down, the bomb is gone. The propaganda is a dead issue."

"Is it? I think not."

Somehow, she had figured an angle and I knew I was sweating. Her smile was as deadly serious as the gun in her hand. I measured the distance to her and thought about Sharon's gun, but each time Lois Hays was following my thoughts as though she could read my mind.

"No," she told us both, "there is not one thing you can do before I kill you. Not one thing."

Trying to play for time, I said, "How can you make it, kid?"

"If you thought about it, you'd see. Tomorrow the papers will carry the story with Duncan Knight's byline and we'll still win. Pity you won't be able to see it."

"What story?"

"How an American citizen carried out an act of unprecedented violence—aided and abetted by authorized agents of this country—and destroyed a harmless Cuban vessel engaged in commerce with a neutral country. Don't you just see how the rest of the world will eat that story up? Oh, I know what you intended the world to think . . . that the *Leona* went down in the midst of a hurricane, and certainly it could be assumed that such an old ship would succumb to hurricane seas. But you're out of luck, Fallon. It will be my story."

"And us?"

"When accused of the act, you tried to take me captive and I had to shoot you both. Who would deny that possibility when they know of the three men lying dead on the wharf. Fallon, you're better off dead. And me, I'll live to work another day. I'll see that my story is well supported and I don't think the government will want to go into the matter any more than is necessary. They want no part of a shooting war."

She smiled again and raised the gun a little higher. "Outside, please. We might as well keep it clean. I don't want any shots heard—not just yet."

She stepped back through the door as we came toward her.

Tuck's words: *There are still some of us left.*

Yes, there were.

We stood in the fierce forefoot of Ingrid, with our clothes snapping around our legs, our faces stung by sand that was ripping by. I held Sharon as tightly as I could and kept walking. Lois was still backing up, almost ready to pull the trigger. We walked forward and kept on walking, the three of us that were left—two in the front and one behind and all the while the crazy scream of the wind was the only sound we could hear.

The gun came up, leveled on the last step Lois took, but in our faces she read that we had won after all. There were still some of us left like Tuck had said, two in front and one behind her.

She started to scream as she backed into the great churning blades of the prop on the Mustang and dissolved into a red, misty froth that was carried away in the gale.